At the end of Prison

Four lawmen surrounded the two women, their laser weapons drawn.

"Stop your unruly activity at once." The lead lawman was itching for some trigger action. "Put your hands above your heads."

Demeter studied them. She knew they hoped for any excuse to vaporize them into piles of smoking bones. She responded by shoving Shike's unconscious body toward them. The lawmen moved in tighter.

"I repeat. Stop your unruly activity at once and put your hands above your head."

Demeter could not tell them apart. They looked and sounded the same. She suspected they all crawled out of the same test tube together. She shared a quick glance with Vesta. The younger woman responded with a knowing wink.

Vesta stomped on the shin of the lawman nearest her and snatched his weapon. Demeter caught another with her elbow and secured his weapon. She fired above their heads.

"Send for the prison transport!" The lead lawman barked into his shoulder comm-radio. "We have two unruly lawbreakers!"

Vesta bludgeoned the officer's forehead with the handle of the laser pistol she snatched. The others jumped on her and wrestled her to the ground. She never stopped fighting them until she heard Demeter's voice.

"Okay, okay. You got us. Take us to the judge."

The struggle ended. A lawman laughed. "I don't know what world you think you're on, chippy." He panted, straining to catch his breath. "There are no judges here. You are going directly to the Prison Planet."

Galaxy Warriors

Special Edition Novelization

by Robert Freese

Based on the screenplay by
Janet Hetherington

Story by Brett Kelly

An  Movie Novelization

Galaxy Warriors: Special Edition Novelization Copyright 2023 by Robert Freese

Script, artwork and photographs Copyright 2021 by Gray Chance Entertainment/Brett Kelly

Special thanks to Brett Kelly and Anne Marie Frigon.

ICFH-MN 002

Published by ItCameFromHollywood LLC
July 2023

This is a work of fiction. All the characters, organizations, and events portrayed in this novel are products of the author's imagination or are used fictitiously. Any resemblance to actual persons, living or dead (except for satirical purposes), is entirely unintentional.

All rights reserved. No portion of this book may be reproduced in any form without permission from the publisher, except as permitted by U.S. copyright law. For permissions, contact: itcamefromhollywood@gmail.com.

Cover Designed by K.C. Redman
Cover Background Image: pikisuperstar on Freepik
itcamefromhollywood.net

An  Movie Novelization

Galaxy Warriors

Special Edition Novelization

Robert Freese

Dedicated with love to my mom.

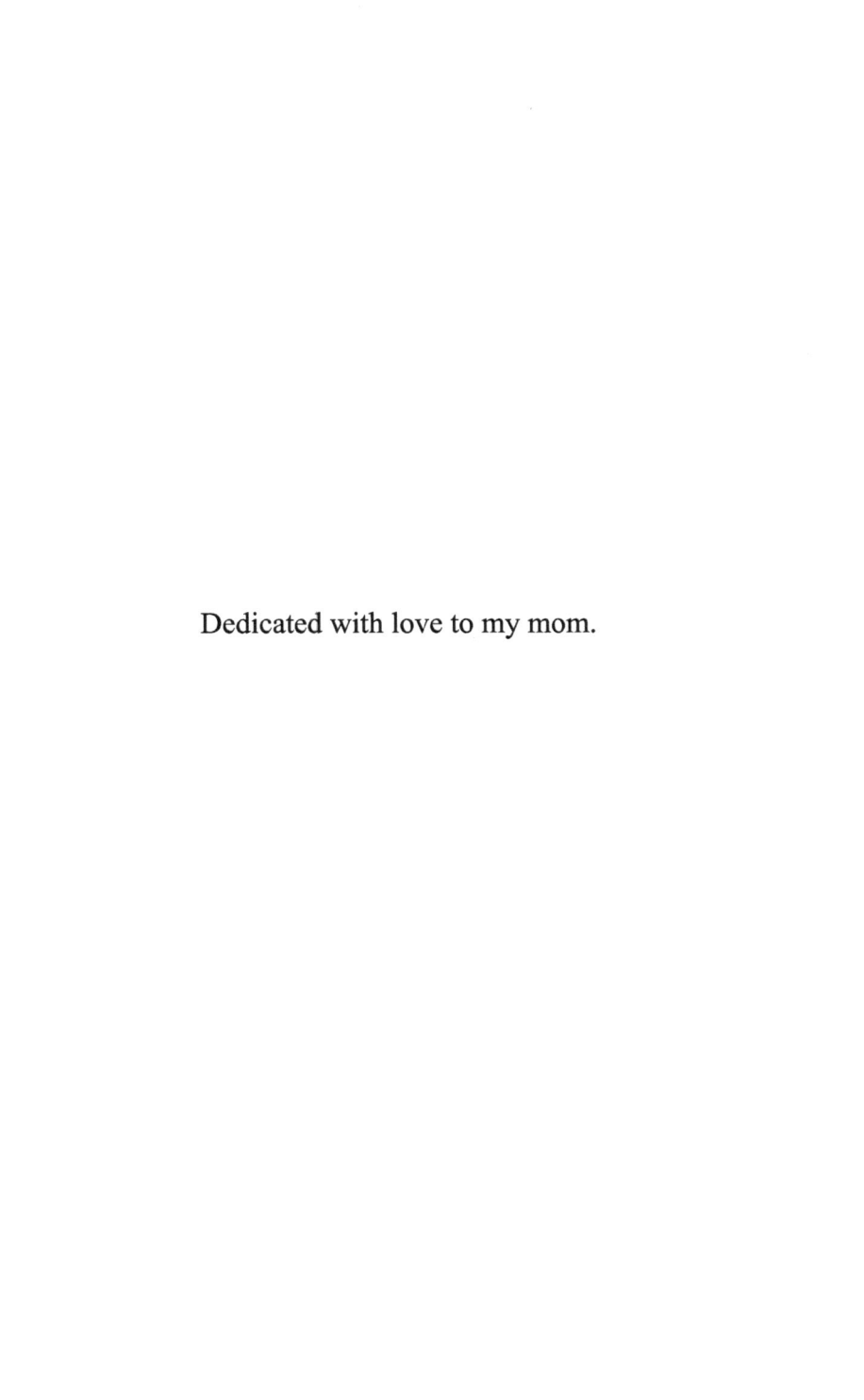

Table of Contents

Chapter 1: Prisoner ----- 3
Chapter 2: Tartarus: Prison Planet----- 7
Chapter 3: Cozzi: Pleasure Planet----- 10
Chapter 4: Escape!----- 19
Chapter 5: Artemis Missing----- 24
Chapter 6: Ruckus on Parbola----- 33
Chapter 7: Mayhem in the Marketplace----- 39
Chapter 8: Welcome to Hell----- 48
Chapter 9: Enyo and the New Warrior----- 52
Chapter 10: Hell Under Multiple Suns----- 55
Chapter 11: Midnight Visits----- 63
Chapter 12: Flight from the Fight Zone----- 67
Chapter 13: The Kill Games---- 75
Chapter 14: Warriors in Chains----- 86
Chapter 15: A Wager----- 91
Chapter 16: Beauty and the Brute-----94
Chapter 17: The Protective Mother----- 98
Chapter 18: A Plan of Action----- 100

Chapter 19: Pair Day----- 104
Chapter 20: The Secrets of Tartarus----- 108
Chapter 21: Sister Battles Sister----- 112
Chapter 22: Beneath Tartarus----- 119
Chapter 23: The Ghost of Tacitus----- 122
Chapter 24: Clash of the Warriors----- 125
Chapter 25: The Destruction of Tartarus----- 129
Chapter 26: Revolt of the Captive Women-----134
Chapter 27: The End of the World----- 138
Chapter 28: Feast of the Pharons----- 142
Chapter 29: A New Regime Arises----- 145
Chapter 30: Score to Settle ----- 149
Chapter 31: Artemis in Peril ----- 152
Chapter 32: The Calm Before the Storm----- 157
Chapter 33: The Good Place----- 160
Chapter 34: Out of Hell, Into the Fire----- 164
Chapter 35: Unruly Bitches! ----- 167
Chapter 36: A Life in the Stars----- 172
A Note from the Writer----- 177
Vintage Lobby Cards----- 182

Chapter 1: Prisoner

She noticed the steady hum rumbling the air around her and awoke.

A song? A lullaby? What was it?

Her mind struggled to identify the melody. Mother? Mother used to hum them to sleep at night when they were still on the planet Crichton, awaiting their father's return. Father was a commander in the Star League.

Father never returned. They never heard from him again. When mother questioned her contacts within the Star League council, she learned nothing. They told her only that father's mission was of strictest confidence, even to spouses. No one could tell her if he was alive or dead.

Sadness filled her heart when she realized it was not mother humming. She knew beyond a doubt. Mother stayed behind on Crichton, having made a deal for Artemis and her sister to have safe transport off-world. She could not find passage before…

Bittersweet memories needled Artemis into consciousness. Fog wrapped her brain, and what she saw when her eyes fluttered open was a world dim and soft around the edges. The humming continued. She struggled toward wakefulness.

Sedatives? Did someone give her a drug? Waves of disorientation broke across her brain. She recognized the cold metal floor beneath her.

Why am I on the floor?

Where am I?

Her last clear memory was leaving the club J-Syn in Barbera's Delta 3 sector after the show. Artemis met friends to hear the band Seven-OH-Seven from Aix play. They were the Kalaa System's hottest new group. They danced all night, through the group's final set, then said their goodbyes and headed back to their quarters. Artemis lived all the way over in Delta 8 sector.

Did someone drug her while she danced with her friends at J-Syn?

Her eyes fluttered open. The world was faint and dreamlike. There was a dim, distant glow above her.

While her surroundings came into focus, the young girl tried to stretch her body to help awaken. A bolt of fear seized her heart. The tips of her fingers touched cold steel, as did the bottoms of her bare feet. She tried curling into a protective position, but found it impossible.

A cold metal cuff secured her right ankle. The restraint connected to a short length of chain anchored to the metal wall. The chain prevented her from drawing in both knees.

Artemis squinted through the murkiness. She forced herself to focus on her surroundings. The humming grew louder, enveloping her senses. It was the only sound drowning out the frantic beating of her heart.

Calm down! Don't panic!

Freaking out would not help her situation one bit.

Four cold metal walls surrounded her. Filth and scribblings covered the walls. The sour scent of a Zariatin hung in the air. Zariatin was a species known for putting off a defensive odor when frightened.

The walls were ten feet tall, with the faraway light bar overhead supplying dull illumination. It could have been a distant star.

Where am I?

She reminded herself again to calm down and not to panic.

Scratched onto the filthy walls were symbols and words. She

read what she understood, but many words and phrases were in languages she did not recognize. What she read made her heart sink further.

Anything is possible, but the odds are astronomically against it, one scribbling read.

Another said, *The time is the tomorrow after tomorrow*, and still another, *Science for the sake of science.*

The outline of a door came into focus. She made a grab for it, but the ankle cuff limited her reach. Artemis squirmed and pushed with the balls of her feet, stretching until she could touch the door's surface. She made a fist and landed a solid blow on the metal surface that echoed throughout the room. She hit the door and heard the echo, and again.

"Help me!"

She pounded the door, crying for help until the effort exhausted her. The strain on her ankle was too much. The cuff bit into her flesh, drawing blood.

There was no response beyond the door. She was alone in the room.

No, she thought, correcting herself. This is not a room. It is a cell. I am a prisoner. Who is my captor?

Why am I here?

What is this place?

Without warning, the dim light above began flashing bright red, like a festering, angry sun. A sharp klaxon rang out, piercing the air, driving all thoughts out of her head.

Hands clapped over her ears, she repeatedly screamed, "Stop it!"

Strobing red light made the walls seem to shudder. In the chaos, Artemis feared they were slowly inching forward, closer, toward her. She knew they would stop only when they touched, her body compacted between them, pressed flat, crushed to bits.

The flashing light revealed a portal window. It seemed very far away from where she lay on the cold floor.

A moment later, mercifully, everything stopped. The flashing red light and the piercing alarm ceased, leaving behind only the cold dark emptiness.

The steady humming continued. She recognized the humming for what it was. Reaction engines.

I'm on a ship!

All the pieces began connecting. Artemis realized she was a captive on an unknown ship, bound for an unknown destination. Fear's icy fingers seized her heart.

The cell shook violently, punctuating her fear. Thrusters propelled the ship forward, gaining speed. The sensation of flight, of acceleration, made her stomach do a somersault. She hated space travel, even though she spent a good part of her life on spaceships and space stations. Had hated it ever since her mother put her and her sister on that escape ship and promised to find them, only to watch horrified when Crichton…

She scrambled to her feet. Another vibration rocked the cell. It threatened to throw her off balance. She stumbled, flapping her arms for balance and remained upright. Legs bent, she waited to absorb another shock. The cuff around her ankle bit deeper into her flesh.

Steady, the vibrations passed. Artemis raised onto the tips of her toes, peered out the window.

A bright flash exploded outside, filled the cell with instant brightness. It blinded her. She turned away. The after-effects made her see blasts of red light all around her. She felt the ship enter the atmosphere.

The vibrations grew more intense. Artemis feared the cell, if not the entire ship, would shake to pieces, and they would burn up before they completed the atmospheric re-entry.

The ship continued its rapid descent to the planet's surface. Vibrations rattled through her body.

"Where are you taking me?" she cried out.

The unknown planet rocketed toward her at an incomprehensible speed.

Then, the door slid open and a dead-eyed guard entered the cell.

Chapter 2:
Tartarus: Prison Planet

Despite the fear gnawing at her stomach, Artemis slept in a protective ball on the metal floor. She drew her knees to her chest and drifted to sleep.

During the last leg of the transfer, guards assembled the captives in a giant holding cell. Bodies crushed together. The transport hull was as filthy as the tiny cell she awoke in. Sweat and fear hung heavy in the air.

It did not take long for the women to learn that their destination was the prison processing center on Tartarus. They muttered, speculating about what processing entailed. They shared horrible stories about Prison Planet. Dead-eyed guards shushed them. A knee to the back was the reward if the mumbling persisted.

None of the women appeared to be the master criminals Artemis thought deserving of banishment to the prison planets. Most looked scared, confused.

She forced herself to close her eyes, unable to keep her mind from wild thoughts of torture or worse. The steady rumble of the transport's turbos swayed her. Blocking out everything around her, she fell into a light sleep. She lost herself in the engine's constant humming, awaking when the ship set down.

Artemis spoke to no one. She kept her eyes from meeting

anyone else. A queasy feeling washed over her.

"On your feet, chippies."

The captain of the guards marched into the cell once the transport landed. His heavy footfalls reverberated throughout the metal hull.

He introduced himself as Rex. She knew he would not hesitate to order his men to deal with them with extreme prejudice if any of them became unruly.

Clad in black armor, he looked menacing. Except for his eyes, a helmet and mask hid his facial features. The eyes were not vacant like his subordinates. The rest of the guards wore red armor. They shared the same lifelessness in their eyes. They were all hooked on the same behavioral meds. The grim-faced guards wore helmets but not masks.

He gripped a coiled whip in one gloved hand. Artemis doubted it took much provocation for Rex to snap the whip into action.

Rex barked, "Prisoners on your feet! We have arrived at the Prison Planet. Line up in an orderly fashion. Each of you will go through processing, followed by cell assignment. Enjoy your stay."

Please, no.

Without a word, prisoners stood and formed a line. Like Artemis, most kept their heads lowered to avoid making any eye contact.

A hydraulic hiss whooshed in the air and the transport hatch opened. Blazing sunlight and dry heat poured into the hull like a blistering flow of lava.

More guards entered the hull through the hatch. They moved among the prisoners, jerking the slower moving women to their feet. Guards shoved them forward.

"Get your hands off of me!" It was one of the young women. Artemis thought her name was Nova. She had overheard her whispering to her friends, Reena and Meagan. Lawmen arrested them on Kuba for no obvious reason. Nova was the most outspoken of the three. Her friends stared at her in wide-eyed shock.

"You will comply and get in line." The captain's voice boomed like the thunder on Juneris. The thunderclaps on Juneris rang out for miles. They shattered the protective shields of dwellings simply from the shock waves they produced. Artemis did not doubt the guard's voice could do the same.

"Let's make a run for it," Nova said. She was excited, not thinking. She looked to her friends for support and then to the other women in the hull. They refused to look her way, let alone join in her halfhearted escape, and she screwed up her face in anger.

Determined to at least try to escape, Nova punched the guard who had jerked her upright on the nose, knocking him a step backwards. His helmet flew off his head. Reena and Meagan screamed for their friend to stop when the guard, Cletus, in one reflexive movement, drew his laser pistol and fired. A red beam of light seized Nova.

She screamed in excruciating pain. Her body hung suspended for a moment within the blast of red laser light. When it was over, a smoldering pile of bones crumbled to the hull floor.

The women gasped. The overpowering stench of charred flesh wafted up and made them sick.

"Prisoners will comply," Rex said. It was not a question.

Drained of any further defiance, the remaining prisoners complied. They formed a line, which the guards put into motion. Artemis tiptoed around the charred remains of Nova, and fell in line.

Brightness met her at the hatch opening, and she hesitated, raising a hand to block out the scorching suns. A desolate landscape surrounded them. The only distinguishing structure on the topography was the prison. It was a large, foreboding mini-city made up of multiple giant domed buildings. Built for only one purpose, it kept prisoners locked inside.

"Keep moving," the dead-eyed guard outside the hatch said, pulling Artemis forward. Her bare feet stepped off the metal hatch door onto the burning sands of Tartarus. Prison Planet. It was good to have ground underfoot, but it was unbearably hot. She hurried to catch up with the other prisoners. The guards led them to the prison processing center.

Head up, sunlight burning hot on her face. As much as she hated to even think the thought, in a desperate, quiet voice she said, "Find me, Demeter. Please find me."

Chapter 3:
Cozzi: Pleasure Planet

Demeter made her way through the throng of bodies. The sidewalks and streets pulsated with life. Galactic beings crowded Cozzi, seeking entertainment. Neon signs flashed like beacons, illuminating the misty night. Music from the pleasure palaces fused into a never-ending chaotic melody. Heard above the traffic choked streets that permeated the sector, it infused the night world with energy. Sidewalk vendors offered food, drink, and games of chance.

Cozzi was a galactic hot spot, a pleasure planet offering something for every taste. Big game hunting, gambling, dangerous sports, nonstop nightlife; simulations the size of small townships offered complete submersion into alternate worlds. Each world was based on a unique time in Earth's history. If ancient Rome caught your fancy, you were in luck. If the Middle Ages were more to your interests, no problem. They offered a prehistoric world filled with long extinct species of primitive creatures. Their most popular destination recreated the ancient American west when it was at its wildest.

Those were only a minute sampling of the pleasures Cozzi offered. One could spend a lifetime on the planet and experience no delight twice.

Demeter entered the Etor sector. The pleasures offered provided a more physical gratification.

Standing six feet in height, Demeter towered over most in the crowd. Her back straight, she moved through the crowd with the confident stride of a warrior. Long, curly auburn locks cascaded off her shoulders. She was one of the most beautiful women in the crush of bodies.

Muscular and fit, Oko armor revealed her sculpted arms. The fabric comprised a lightweight polymer-mesh material formed over the specific contours of her body. The material fit like a second skin. It shielded the wearer from most weapons, excluding those fired at close range. It also kept her body at a steady thermal temperature.

"Anything yet?" Vesta, her partner and pilot of her ship, the Wolfhound, said in her ear-comm. She knew Vesta tracked her every move. She provided Demeter with an extra pair of eyes.

"Negative. This creep could be anywhere," she reported back. No one in the crowd paid her any attention. Everyone focused on getting from one place to another. She continued her journey. Her boots splashed along the rain-soaked sidewalk.

Sometime later, she stopped walking and stepped into a side alley. The Pag tracker pinged loudly. The alley was dank and smelled of spoiled meat and used alcohol. Before freeing the tracker from its holster, she heard something nearby belch. She spun; laser pistol drawn. Demeter was on high alert, ready for anything.

It was an old wino. His complexion a dull purple tint speckled with red splotches. She could not determine what planet he originated from. All the blood vessels in his nose had long burst. He sat against a building, murmuring a tune, and smiling. Beside him stood a mechanical Robodog. The robotic dog, out of date and covered in grime, had seen better days. It stood still, rusted stiff, except for its tail, which wagged noisily, in dire need of lubricating oil.

The wino chugged from his bottle of Klytus. The blue liquid went down smoothly. She saw the warm cerulean glow it brought to his rheumy eyes. He wiped his mouth with the back of a dirty hand. He blinked once, then a second time, and suddenly noticed Demeter standing there.

His dirty eyeballs examined her from head to toe. A drunken smile stretched across his face.

"Nice boots, chief. Nice boots."

"Scat you old rummy, before I put the two of you in that bottle." She nodded at the bottle in his shaky grip.

The wino took offense to her harsh words and struggled to pull himself upright.

Unable to tell by looking, he had once been a space adventurer not unlike herself. The time had long passed since the galaxy knew him as the "Madman of the Stars." He had a life of unending adventure. Younger, the man spent more than half his lifetime exploring infinite space. He prevailed over every escapade the universe put forth. His loyal Robodog at his side always. Despite his life of adventure, all the beings he met and helped and the tales he had to tell, he still grew old and weak. Every part of him hurt. The Klytus helped dull the pain and the memories.

"I'm walking. I'm walking." He coughed once and painfully crawled up the wall to his feet. He mumbled, "Some people. This is my home. Come barging in like they own everything. This is my home, and I wasn't bothering not a soul. Just enjoying a nightcap." He belched again.

Demeter tried not to giggle. The old man checked his pockets repeatedly, patting frantically until he located another bottle of the blue liquor. He smiled. "Ok, I'm all packed up."

He looked down at the little Robodog. "Come on, Kip. Time to find us a new home."

The robotic dog actually barked once, but it sounded more like a hollow, mechanical cough. It was sad. Demeter watched Kip follow the wino, both on busted legs, out onto the crowded sidewalk.

Palming the Pag tracker, it beeped steadily. A green button blinked beneath the screen. She pressed it, activating the map feature.

Above the screen's surface appeared a holographic, three-dimensional image. The three-square blocks in the Pag's range appeared. The center of the holographic topography blinked red.

"Zoom in," she commanded, and the tracker responded. The holographic city zoomed forward. The red blip filled the holo-field, forming an image. An ugly face took shape. It was her prey.

Kryll.

The three-dimensional holograph recreated the official wanted communique issued, along with Kryll's arrest warrant. The holographic image of his head and shoulders rotated slowly. She noted all the details. Beady eyes, unkempt shag of hair, rotten teeth, and a crooked nose, broken but never properly set.

The holographic image shimmered and changed. It delivered a full body rundown which highlighted scars, birthmarks and two tattoos. A prison identification code on the back of his left hand read, "PSP-2758." The second, on his right forearm, depicted the scantily armored Valkyrie Saint-Exmin in a compromising position.

His list of crimes read like a "greatest hits" package for career dirtbags. He committed every crime from petty larceny to forging Megacredits. His current offenses included pushing RADIC-Q-Z as a miracle drug capable of fixing whatever troubled the user. Untested, a single drop on the user's tongue offered an instant euphoric sensation. It actually made the user feel acutely reinvigorated. The drug's major downside, it made the user an addict for life after a couple hits. The user spent the rest of their life seeking that euphoric sensation. Too much RADIC-Q-Z could erase the user's mind as easily as erasing a vid-screen cassette tape. Once wiped clean, they had less intelligence than a newly hatched Leemoid.

Demeter never played judge or jury to the fugitives she pursued, but for what came down to a filthy drug peddler, she felt zero sympathy. Few criminals were lower than a creep who sold any substance that could be harmful to another living being.

She wanted to wipe up the wet streets with the scumbag.

"Something?" It was Vesta's voice.

"Oh, yeah. I got him, and he's one ugly creep." She entered a code into the tracker and hit the "send" button.

After a moment, Vesta responded.

"Got it."

Demeter heard Vesta's fast typing on the bridge of the Wolfhound. The clicking continued for a long moment before the pilot spoke again.

What is taking so long?

"I have a lock on him. He's less than a quarter of a click southwest of your location. It looks like…" Her voice trailed off. Demeter heard more of the rapid tapping of computer keys.

"Do you see… Emeralida's Fun House of Delights?"

Across the street, the vibrant pink neon sign announcing Emeralida's Fun House of Delights buzzed in the murky night. Its brilliant colors reflected off the wet street below. Underneath the sign was a giant second story picture window revealing the fun house's plush interior.

"Yeah, I got it." A look of determination set into her brow.

"Ok... now," Vesta started hesitantly. Her voice was gentle but steadfast. "I need you to remember that you don't go in there, fists blazing. The Space Service on Cozzi is heavy. They take their peacekeeping duties seriously. It won't be like that time on Kobol..."

Demeter was not listening. She strode purposefully into the slow-moving traffic. She directed all her focus toward the building with the giant pink neon sign. Nothing would get in her way.

An all-terrain 8-wheel transport scrambler screeched to a stop to avoid careening into her. She did not notice. The driver yelled at her in a language she did not understand. The gist of his outburst was easy enough to interpret when coupled with his furious hand gestures.

She pushed through the shiny chrome swinging doors, entering the elegantly decorated antechamber. Crimson curtains hung from the high reaching ceiling. Finely crafted sculptures and artwork were on display. A fountain spouting a crystalline azure liquid centered before a grand stairwell. The stairs led up into all the decadent playrooms Emeralida's offered. Lit from within, the shimmering water had an effervescent glow. The grandest, most elegant chandelier she had ever seen hovered over the center of the room and shined cool, seductive slivers of light in every direction.

A beautiful female Jilllucian greeted her. The woman wore a flowing robe of fuchsia, adorned with sparkling amethyst symbols. Symbols representing pleasure in various languages shimmered. The robe did little to conceal the supple emerald flesh and feminine figure underneath. "Welcome to Emeralida's," she said in a smooth voice that tingled in Demeter's ears. "I am Meia Long. How may we serve your needs tonight?"

"I'm looking for a man."

Meia smiled. "We have many fine gentlemen, of all types, to choose from." With a quick flick of her wrist, she summoned a virtual menu of men of all shapes, sizes, and colors for her to peruse.

Demeter almost blushed.

"I'm not looking for a gentleman. I'm looking for a creep."

She activated the Pag tracker. Kryll's holographic image appeared.

The emerald skinned woman shuddered. Her cheeks took on a sour pallor of green.

"A very distinctive man," Meia said.

Before either woman said another word, a scream from upstairs filled the antechamber.

Got him!

"Thanks," Demeter said with a knowing smile and a nod. In a quick movement, she returned the tracker to its holster and bounded up the stairwell. Two plush runners at a time.

A group of costumed revelers stood in shocked silence at the end of the right hallway. They peered and pointed with expressions of disgust into the grand playroom. Demeter ran down the hall.

"What's happening?" Vesta asked.

Demeter ignored her partner for the moment. She pushed through the bodies and entered.

The playroom was humongous and decorated like an old-fashioned dance hall. On a raised stage sat a band of retro clockwork automatons. Each continued playing its instrument, even though the dancing stopped.

Chaos spread through the celebrants.

A woman on the floor screamed. Someone stole her bejeweled waist chain. The raucous crowd searched for the culprit. The woman repeated her story. From her costume, Demeter doubted she was a doctor or medical attendant of any sort. The stethoscope around her neck made up the entirety of her costume.

She noticed how suggestive all the costumes were. Most revelers wore variations of standard service uniforms, but none were proper for any type of medical, law enforcement or military service.

Beyond the fray, she saw a man running. He hit the side door hard, pushing it open with a loud bang.

"Kryll," she said and bolted after him.

Through the door, she chased him down another long hallway

and into another grand playroom. Entering, tropical heat enveloped her. The humidity suggested an actual sun filling the room.

She chased the fugitive around the perimeter of a vast swimming pool. Bodies, devoid of anything but the tiniest scrap of fabric, lounged about lazily. Laughing transformed into screaming when Kryll barreled through the sanctuary. The people Kryll didn't push into the pool or onto the laps of other sunbathers, Demeter did. The only difference was the hasty apology Demeter yelled behind her.

Are those even bathing suits?

She wondered why someone spent their wealth on such silly extravagance, but not for long. She stayed focused on snatching Kryll before he slipped away.

He slammed through another door and hurried down another long hallway. Demeter was not far behind.

"Stop right now, Kryll and I'll go easy on you!"

"You wish, chippy," he yelled back, ducking to his left.

How big is this place?

The outside of the joint was deceiving. It really was a fun house. She followed close behind, tracking his heavy footfalls and labored breathing.

"I have thermals on both of you now. What's going on?" Vesta watched the action on her vid-screen.

"Dancing. Dinner. He's showing me a good time." Demeter dashed after him into the other room.

She raced down an endless row of lockers. Steam billowed from showers beyond the lockers. Laser showers blasted refreshing rays of warm, cleansing light. The further she ran into the changing room, the quicker she lost her bearings, becoming more discombobulated.

Metal locker doors banged shut. A man's voice bellowed nearby. "What do you think you're doing?"

"Get out of my way!"

Kryll must have lost his way, too.

Demeter closed her eyes, focused, and followed the scuffle between the two men.

"Stop!" She saw his shape through the mist.

Kryll stood over a man splayed across the tile floor. The man was defenseless, wearing only a towel around his waist.

Kryll's oversized boot hovered over the man's head, ready to stomp. He froze when Demeter materialized from the steam.

"Make it easy on yourself and don't make me drag your ugly hide back to my ship," she said.

"What's happening?" The pilot's voice chirped in her ear.

No response.

Not good, Vesta thought. It was never good when Demeter refused to respond.

"I hear something. I know I hear something. Are you hurting anyone, Demeter? Hello?"

"You don't have me yet, chippy." Kryll turned, disappearing into the thick tendrils of steam.

"You've got to be kidding me." Demeter wanted to scream. She sighed instead.

"Go get him," the man said. Adrenaline coursed through his body after the altercation with Kryll.

"Are you okay?"

He shrugged. "My pride is a little bruised, but I'll be fine."

She smiled. He winked back. Her face flushed for only a moment, then she continued her pursuit. She followed Kryll to the end of the steam filled changing room, down another hallway.

She saw the giant plate glass window at the far end of the hallway. Neon blasts of pink light blinked outside. It was the second story window facing the street, the front of Emeralida's Fun House of Delights.

Kryll did not slow down. His legs pumped, building speed the closer he got to the window.

"Don't think about it, creep." She knew it was futile, but she felt obligated to say something.

"See you in the Forbidden Zone, chippy!"

Driving his leg muscles for everything they were worth, he launched his gigantic frame into the center of the window, its weakest point.

Unable to look away, Demeter watched with a giant grin.

Kryll slammed into the window with a resounding thud. The force threw him backwards fifteen feet. The sound echoed down the hallway.

Demeter winced, feeling every bit of the impact.

"What was that? It sounded horrible."

"You heard that?" Demeter slowed to an even pace, walking toward Kryll's lifeless form. The creep wasn't going anywhere.

The pilot said, "It sounded like booster rockets conking out and exploding."

"It was something like that," Demeter said. She grinned sideways down at the inert body at her feet.

She squatted and rolled him onto his back. He struggled to hold on to consciousness. The world spun around him.

Demeter returned him to the prone position. She jerked his arms behind him with little concern for his comfort, securing his wrists with zip cuffs. The big man moaned pitifully.

"You know something, Kryll. I've seen all kinds of stupid stunts in my life, but that one jumped to the top spot on my all-time favorite stupid stunts list." She laughed, then pulled the brute onto his shaky legs.

"Come on, big boy. Jeb is waiting to meet you." She pushed him down the corridor.

A wave of dizziness overcame Kryll. He wobbled. His head throbbed. Demeter shoved him forward.

Chapter 4: Escape!

Demeter escorted Kryll down the grand stairwell into the antechamber. Meia Long approached the bounty hunter. The delicate green skinned beauty asked if she found Emeralida's accommodations pleasing.

"It was a visit I won't soon forget." Demeter nodded.

The Jillucian bowed and smiled.

"Let's go." She shoved Kryll forward.

"Thank you."

A masculine voice. Behind her.

She stopped, turned around. The man from the laser showers stood before her. He looked different, fully dressed, not wrapped in a towel. Her heart fluttered. Without the obscuring wisps of steam, he was handsome in every way possible.

Her face grew warm. Demeter hoped no one noticed in the beams of soft light.

"How's that bruised pride?" She offered an awkward smile. Inwardly, she regretted saying anything.

Shut up, Demeter. Stay focused on the fugitive. There's a bounty to collect.

To her surprise, he answered. "I feel a lot better now, thanks to you."

"You look a lot better."

What? Stop saying words, Demeter!

He smiled. His eyes lit up.

She could not help herself. She enjoyed every pleasing inch of him. Through his tight-fitting garments, she made out the ripped physique only hinted at in the laser showers. Sharp features, firm jaw, crystal blue eyes and wavy blonde hair topped off the package.

In addition, it surprised her to see that he was at least an inch taller than her. That was something rare in the galaxy. She noticed the men she met were always short. Demeter suspected it had something to do with space travel and variable gravitational forces on the male skeleton. She believed it altered some bodies, but that was her own theory.

"I like your smile," he said.

"Somebody, please kill me now." Kryll sounded disgusted.

Demeter grabbed him by the scruff of his neck and shook him.

"Shut your mouth-hole, grease-ball!"

"I can see you're busy," the man said.

"Yeah, a little." She peered into his blue eyes, lost for a moment.

"Can we get on with this?" Kryll flinched when Demeter glared his way.

"Do you frequent Astron Belt?" he asked. Demeter liked the way the soft overhead light beams sparkled in his eyes.

"From time to time," she said. Her hardened exterior softened.

Is he hitting on me in the middle of apprehending a fugitive?

Her cheeks flushed.

"What's going on?"

Demeter ignored the voice in her ear. She forgot Vesta and the Wolfhound completely.

"Maybe we can catch up when you're not so busy." His smile made her heart melt.

"Maybe we could catch up when I'm not so busy," she said. Terror seized her.

Did I just parrot everything he just said?

He chuckled. "My name's Dexter. I work in the Borf building at Digital Leisure. I look forward to taking you out for a drink."

"I'd like that." Demeter memorized every line and feature on his face. It was the same process in which she burned the image of a fugitive's face into her memory.

"I want a drink," Kryll said. He appeared nauseated by the bounty hunter's inept flirting.

"If you don't want the remnants of your teeth rolling across the concrete, zip it!" She shook Kryll for emphasis.

"What's your name?" Dexter asked when she looked back at him.

"Demeter."

All at once, a look of recognition and excitement flashed across his face. She knew the look well. She despised the look.

Her heart sank.

That is the end of that conversation.

His smile grew even bigger.

Here it comes.

"Wait... Demeter? As in *the* Demeter? The one and only Demeter? Demeter, the galaxy famous bounty hunter?"

"Yeah," she said. She responded with little interest and more than a pinch of resentment. She wished Vesta would intervene. Anything. But her partner kept quiet.

Kryll noticed the change in the bounty hunter's demeanor. Her sudden discomfort and embarrassment amused him to no end.

"I've heard of you, of course. You are taller than I thought you'd be. I never thought I'd ever get to meet you in real life."

Demeter tried to smile but bit the inside of her cheek instead. Feelings of rejection running over her, she pushed Kryll through the swinging doors. On the sidewalk outside, she surveyed their surroundings. It did not appear anyone planned to give her any problems.

"Can I call you?" he entreated, following her.

"Sure. Yeah. I'm in the, uh, network." She gave him a last glance. He was cute. Very cute. She pushed Kryll along the rain soaked sidewalk, leaving Dexter behind.

"Is that your new boyfriend?" Kryll snickered. When she didn't answer, he taunted her further, asking again, only louder. A wretched smirk infected his warty face.

She shoved him. The wind picked up. Demeter noticed how horrible the creep smelled. Like he had been rolling around in the garbage pits of Pluton. It somehow made everything worse.

Demeter bit her tongue, did her best to ignore him. She wanted to disappear, but she felt like everyone around them watched her every move.

Of course, no one ever recognized her as an attractive woman. No one considered her being attracted to a man. No. She was "Demeter, the famous bounty hunter." Her reputation as a top bounty hunter preceded her wherever she went, overshadowing the fact that was a woman.

"Vesta, I'm heading to the transport pad for pickup."

"Roger." The pilot responded, flipping toggles. Her tone let the bounty hunter know she heard everything. She knew the thoughts in her partner's mind.

It would be nice to one day meet someone oblivious to who I am.

Lost in her thoughts, she paid no attention when Kryll said he had to go to the bathroom. She wanted to knock him out, drag him to the transport in silence.

"Say again, creep?"

Stars erupted before her eyes. An immediate rush of pain shot up her nose and into her head. Waves of pain erupted throughout her skull and her eyes filled with tears. Before she realized Kryll head-butted her, he was out of her grip and then out of her reach.

"No!"

The pain rippled through her skull and she wiped tears from her eyes. She saw Kryll duck down a side street toward the transport pad.

"Vesta! Come in."

She shook off the pain and pushed through the crowd, darting after him.

Nice going, famous bounty hunter!

"What's going on, Demeter?"

"He got away."

"How?"

"Never mind. He's headed toward the transport pad. Get a lock on him before we lose him in the Forbidden Zone."

She raced down the street and reached the transport pad in time to see Kryll's shuttle, Hammerhead, take flight. Boosters fired, preparing for a quick vault into space followed by a warp jump into the Forbidden Zone.

A humanoid pad manager smoking a cigar and carrying a digital clipboard yelled at the Hammerhead for taking off without proper clearance. He shook the clipboard over his head.

Vesta approached with the Wolfhound ready to pick up Demeter. She navigated the craft onto the pad. She neglected reporting in and waiting for clearance before landing illegally.

On the comm-screen she saw the pad manager look away from the Hammerhead and start yelling at her around the cigar. She smiled.

He threw his clipboard at the Wolfhound. A steady stream of silent curses flowed from him without pause.

"Like I can even hear what you're saying," she said and giggled.

An indicator light blinked rapidly when she touched down on the pad. She watched it, looked back at the comm-screen.

"Sorry," Vesta said and shrugged. She completed the landing and released the hatch lock. "I'll only be here for a minute Mr. Screaming-at-everyone-with-a-stinky-cigar-in-his-mouth."

The screen showed the humanoid shaking a fist in the air. She pictured him yelling more curses about her landing the space rig on his pad without permission.

Vesta giggled again at the man's antics. She heard the pressure release on the hatch door hiss open and then slam shut. Forgetting the angry humanoid, she began punching buttons for takeoff.

Chapter 5:
Artemis Missing

Vesta saw the verification, the hatch was secured. Demeter was on board.

She punched in the coordinates, locking on the Hammerhead's flight pattern. The Wolfhound's boosters came to life. Demeter knew the drill. She was holding onto something, safe until the Wolfhound blasted through the outer layer of Cozzi's atmosphere.

Vesta thought Demeter's just-by-the-skin-of-her-teeth escapades were becoming routine. Demeter seemed addicted to the adrenaline constant danger provided. Her schemes never worked as planned, but somehow they always worked out. She kept them one step ahead of the Great Reaper.

Regardless, Vesta trusted the auburn-haired warrior with her life. Demeter found her after a Gynoid raid when she was just a teenager. They decimated her village in the attack. They killed her entire family. In a moment of hopelessness, Demeter appeared. She was four years older than Vesta. The younger woman admired her. Demeter took Vesta with her, kept her from retreating into despair and gave her a new purpose.

When Demeter recognized Vesta's talent for piloting various small ships at a young age, she sent her to flight training. She made sure she received all certifications. Vesta graduated with an Alpha Class Freighter pilot's license. Everything Vesta had she owed to Demeter.

Although they were partners, Vesta admired Demeter like an older sister. In fact, with auburn hair just a shade brighter than Demeter's own curly locks, most people assumed they were sisters.

Demeter had a sister, Artemis. Still, Vesta gave her the respect a younger sibling shows an older.

She locked on the Hammerhead's coordinates. Demeter appeared on the bridge beside her. She punched in a sequence of symbols and the comm-screen revealed Kryll's ugly visage. When he realized the bounty hunters were watching him, he waved, gave them an obscene finger gesture, and offered a smile of chipped, rotten teeth. Demeter noticed he broke through the zip cuffs. Half of the cuffs hung from each wrist.

Did he chew through them with that nasty set of choppers?

"You might as well come in, Kryll. We're going to catch you, no doubt about it." Demeter's nose still ached from his earlier deception. It was nothing less than a sucker punch. It reminded her of her moment of weakness, which made it hurt all the worse.

"Forget about it, Demeter. You'll never outrun my ship. I'm smaller and faster than you." He was gloating, confident.

"You're definitely smaller."

I'm tired of this nonsense.

Demeter wanted this to be over. She needed a laser shower and some bunk time. Her feet were killing her.

To her partner, she said, "Is he really faster than us, Vesta?"

"For the moment. But he's never raced me before." Her eyes left the tracking monitor only to check their coordinates. The Hammerhead made no move without Vesta countering the action beforehand. Her fingers tapped the keyboard at a frantic pace. She entered symbols, sequences, codes and commands, and the Wolfhound responded to each command.

Smug, Kryll said, "If you want to collect the bounty on me, you can't shoot me out of the sky. But I can shoot you!"

Chuckling, he punched a button just out of view and the Hammerhead fired a rear missile directly into the Wolfhound's path. Demeter recognized the missile as a D.B. It stood for Death Blossom. In a matter of seconds, the Wolfhound would be nothing but a puff of space debris and micro dust.

"Dodge it, Vesta!"

"I'm already on it!" Tensing, Vesta gripped the navigational joystick tightly with both hands. She forced the Wolfhound into a sudden sharp dip and spin. Amazingly, the missile stayed locked onto its target.

"It's almost on us," Demeter yelled.

"Yelling is not helping," Vesta shot back. "But this will!" She jerked the joystick a hard right, and the Wolfhound bucked violently. The action nearly sent Demeter tumbling to the bridge floor.

"What the…" Demeter said. She grabbed the navigational console to steady herself.

"Buckle up, I'm making a pretzel twist!" Waiting until the last moment to react, the missile on top of them, Vesta jerked the joystick. The ship's flight path turned a sharp left and then right. Her entire body jerked with the controller. The spaceship made an aerial knot, twisting away and back in, evading the missile.

The Death Blossom passed close enough to singe the Wolfhound's outer shielding. Luckily, it posed no other danger than ruining an already long ruined paint job. It blasted into a passing asteroid, exploding upon contact. The aftershocks from the blast rocked the Wolfhound, but Vesta kept the ship steady.

"That was close." Demeter's eyes returned to Kryll's image on the comm-screen.

"But it worked." Vesta wore a satisfied smile. "And you're welcome."

"That wasn't nice, Kryll. We just want the bounty…" Her voice tapered off. She struggled for something non-confrontational to say. "We don't want to hurt you. Although I'm changing my mind about that."

"Forget it, Demeter. I'm done toying with you. I'm out of here."

The comm-screen erupted into static.

"What does he mean?" Demeter reached past Vesta, pushing buttons, attempting to get the creep back on the comm-screen, but he was jamming the signal.

"My guess, warp jump. If he does that, we'll never get him."

Demeter bit her bottom lip. Blame it on Dexter. If only his stupid muscles, his stupid blonde hair, his stupid gorgeous blue eyes, and his stupid smile hadn't distracted her. Kryll would otherwise be in the brig chilling. She would have her boots kicked off, relaxing on her bunk.

"Unacceptable. How long until this warp jump?"

Fingers clicked atop the keyboard. Symbols and numbers flashed across the screen. "Around twenty seconds."

"Can you lock onto his life-signs?"

Vesta made a face. Did she hear that correctly?

"You're not serious. At these speeds and the warp jump…"

"You bet I am," Demeter said.

Calculations for locking onto Kryll's life signs and transporting him flashed through Vesta's mind. Her brain sent commands that flowed rapidly down her arms and through her fingertips. They tapped coordinates onto the keyboard in a flash. Her eyes scanned all the information blinking on the monitor. There were no guarantees it would work. Hardly. There could be deadly and messy consequences. If the Hammerhead blasted into warp jump a nanosecond sooner than Vesta calculated, only half of Kryll would appear on the Wolfhound. The transportation process would rip him in half between the ships.

"He'll be moving too fast." She shook her head. "All I can do is guess on where his ship will be when I activate the transport command."

Demeter nodded. Her eyes watched the Hammerhead on the tracking screen.

Vesta frowned but prepared the coordinates.

I know Demeter hates to lose a perp, but this is reckless and insane!

The younger woman kept the opinion to herself. She dared not voice her concern, or Demeter might really produce a doozy of a follow-up plan.

"It's that or nothing." Stubborn determination colored Demeter's words.

Resigned to follow her partner's plan of action, Vesta sighed. "Never a dull moment flying with you, Demeter."

She entered the coordinates.

The computer buzzed.

"Count me down," Demeter said. Her eyes never left the vid-screen tracking the Hammerhead.

With a balled fist, Demeter smashed the vid-communication

button on the console. The unexpected action startled Vesta, and she jumped in her seat. The static on the comm-screen crackled and Kryll's ugly face came into focus. He looked surprised.

"Hey, Kryll."

He frowned. "Hey, Demeter. Get ready to eat cosmic dust."

"I have a feeling we'll be seeing each other again real soon." To Vesta she said, "Have him sent directly to the brig."

"No way, Demeter. I'm out of here in five…" he growled.

"Four, three, two, one… now!" Vesta exclaimed. She threw the locking toggle at the precise moment the Hammerhead exploded into a million points of light, vanishing into the Forbidden Zone. At the same moment, Kryll's image disappeared from the comm-screen in an explosion of multi-colored specks of light.

Vesta entered codes, pushed the blinking green button on the navigational console and checked the results. A girlish grin filled her face.

"We got him! He's sitting in our brig as we speak." She felt immense pride in her abilities as a pilot at that moment.

"And his ship?" Demeter asked.

"It is reappearing in the Forbidden Zone, light years from here, with no one on board." She turned to Demeter.

Before enjoying the spoils of a successful capture, the Wolfhound received a hailing signal. Vesta responded.

"Call coming in, partner," she said. She opened the incoming communication.

"Who is it?"

"Jeb."

"Funny. I didn't expect him to be in this quadrant. Put him on."

Jeb Deering appeared on the comm-screen after a crackle of static. He was stoic, as was his usual sunny disposition.

Jeb had been in law enforcement almost his entire life. He joked that each criminal he apprehended over the years created a new gray hair on his head. Thinning hair revealed more of his scalp every day.

The older man knew Demeter since she was a kid. At one time, he thought she would join the Space Service's branch of galactic law enforcement. Her need for adventure took her down a different path. He took her under his wing after she and her sister escaped on that last ship from Crichton. Excelling in personal protection and tracking, she was remarkably efficient at problem solving at a young age. She possessed a confidence that overrode her ability to reason properly. He considered it her most destructive detriment. She considered it her most useful attribute.

Demeter noticed he did not seem like his usual self, but let it pass without comment.

"Hey, Jeb. I was going to call you. We have Kryll in our brig and we want to collect the bounty on him. Have our money ready."

"Oh, that's good." The older man appeared disconnected, out of sorts.

"I thought catching this creep would get a better reaction than that," she said. Demeter expected Jeb to elaborate on why capturing the galaxy's most pursued dope peddler wasn't a bigger deal.

"Sorry, Demeter. I have news for you... not good, I'm afraid." His features grew grim.

"Spill it," Demeter said.

"It's your sister, Artemis."

"Artemis?" Her muscles tensed. "Last I heard, she was on Pyron waiting tables at a tavern."

"Yeah, about that." He grew older with every word. "I received word that she traveled to the planet Barbera. I'm still keeping watch on her, as per our agreement."

"To make sure my enemies aren't gunning for her," Demeter said. She said it for the benefit of reminding Jeb the whole reason she had left Artemis's well-being in his care.

"Yeah." After an uncomfortable silence, the words rushed out of Jeb's mouth like they tasted sour. "Here it is. I lost her personal beacon two days ago."

"What does that mean, you lost her beacon?" Her tone grew sharper on each new syllable. "Is she dead?"

"No, no," he replied too quickly to be reassuring. "I don't think so. If she were dead, I would have received a cease-function signal. Solar flares could mask the beacon or deactivate it or something. She has just... disappeared."

So many thoughts raced through her mind at once. Demeter was at a loss for words.

"Sorry, Demeter," he said.

"Do you have any leads?" Vesta asked. She noticed a slight tremble running through Demeter's crossed arms. Her knuckles cracked. She made tight nervous fists, then flexed her fingers outward.

Jeb tried backpedaling. "I shouldn't even be alerting you to this. I'm a lawman and…"

"We're not," Demeter interrupted.

"The universe has not been kind to your family," Jeb whispered.

"Can you at least send us what intel you have?" Demeter tried speaking as calmly as possible, but she could feel the anger boiling within her. She wanted to drive a fist through the comm-screen monitor. She wanted Jeb's image to go away. "We'll look for Artemis ourselves."

"I strongly suggest you let the local authorities on Barbera look into the matter," he said. His words were stern, but he knew they were useless.

"Yeah, right? If you think I'm trusting the safety of my sister to law flunkies, you've been smoking what Kryll's been peddling."

Jeb selected his words carefully before speaking. "One word of advice, Demeter. Stay out of the way of any local investigation."

Although he was only looking out for her safety, his words seemed petty and condescending. Her knuckles popped. She continued making tight fists until she grabbed the edge of the navigational console and leaned toward the comm-screen. She wanted to make sure Jeb heard her loud and clear. One eyebrow cocked. Her jaw barely moved as she spoke.

"Here are my words of advice; they better stay out of my way."

Jeb was thankful he was safe on his own ship. He cleared his throat.

"What about Kryll?" He looked from Demeter to Vesta.

"Trade you," Vesta said.

He looked relieved to talk about anything else.

"I'll transport Kryll to you and you can transport the money to us. Easy-peasy."

Jeb nodded confirmation of the trade, and Vesta entered the code.

In the brig, Kryll sat quietly, holding his stomach. Being dematerialized and transported before the warp jump caused him considerable severe intestinal discomfort. His stomach wheezed, popped and spasmed. He couldn't have felt worse if he had chugged a case of that rotgut, Klytus. He wished he had a pinch of the RADIC-Q-Z stash to make the pain go away. Whatever drugs he had disappeared with the Hammerhead. Everything he ever owned now floated freely in the Forbidden Zone for any wild pack of Zoners to find and claim as salvage.

The familiar tickling of the dematerialization process intruded upon his thoughts. It touched the center of his queasy stomach and quickly filled his entire being.

"Not again…" he said.

In a flash of multicolored light particles, he was gone. The Wolfhound's brig was empty.

Jeb read a vid-screen to his left. Confirmation of prisoner receival showed on screen. "Bounty received." He quickly punched blinking buttons of assorted colors. "Mega-credits transferred."

"Acknowledged," Vesta responded.

"I hope you find Artemis," Jeb said. His tone was apologetic, but he did not elaborate further.

"If I don't, there will be hell to pay. Demeter out." She punched the vid-communication button. Jeb's image blinked out with a blast of static, replaced by a map of the stars and constellations.

"Are you okay?"

"I will be… when I find my sister. I…" Her voice cracked, and she went silent. She turned away.

"What," Vesta prodded softly.

"I have a zillion enemies. If any of them laid a finger on her, so help me…" Her voice tapered off. The overwhelming desire to find her sister and unleash a fury of vengeance on those enemies, whoever they were, made her blood boil.

"Not true," Vesta said.

"What?" The comment pried her from her brooding reverie of revenge. She turned to look at the pilot.

"You have maybe a million enemies and some of them are mine," Vesta said. She smiled.

Demeter gazed at the star map and fought the urge to smirk even a little in the presence of her junior partner. She knew her desire for revenge clouded her thinking. The only important matter was locating

Artemis and getting her back safely.

"Get us to the Barbera system," she said.

"En route, partner."

Keys clicked furiously atop the keyboard and the Wolfhound's engines came to life with a roar. Fire erupted from the boosters. The ship blasted toward their new destination.

Chapter 6:
Ruckus on Parbola

Demeter sat in the co-pilot's seat, her feet propped on the Wolfhound's navigational console, lost in thought. She tapped the directional joystick with the scuffed toe of her boot and rubbed her wrist.

How did this happen? How did Artemis vanish?

As the older sister, Demeter swore to their mother to protect her baby sister and always keep her safe. Currently, she did not know where Artemis was. It frustrated her.

After escaping Crichton, the sisters and the other refugees found temporary lodging on the Hephastus space station. The station offered sanctuary while they awaited assignment to off-world colonies. It was a time of significant expansion throughout the universe. Searching for a better world and a new life was common among colonists.

The Hephastus harbored too many people. Limited food and sleeping quarters created problems. Constant noise and chaos made the accommodations downright depressing.

In no time, Demeter became an effective pick-pocketer. She preyed on station personnel and workers she knew made a steady income. She honed her skills. Mega-credits stolen from the workers enabled her to buy better food and even blankets to keep them warm at night.

It was only after she tried picking the pocket of off-duty security officer Jeb Deering that Demeter met her match. Jeb apprehended her before she could count the stolen credits.

She never experienced fear, and she showed nothing but resistance when Jeb snatched her with his credit folder in her tiny hands. She had nothing but bad attitude and stubbornness to spare. Artemis, however, was close to tears. He took them back to the station's holding cells. Language not fit for a child poured out of Demeter the entire way.

Jeb soon realized he would never scare the auburn-haired girl straight. She was not like other kids. Pure survival instinct overrode all her other emotions.

Beaten, but determined not to admit it, Jeb Deering tried another tactic. He bought them a meal in the security officer's cafeteria. They filled their bellies until they almost popped. When they could eat no more, he ordered bowls scooped high with smooth Brescia Cream covered in hot fudge sauce.

After her little sister satisfied her hunger, Demeter calmed down. She never relaxed or let her guard down. She stayed on full alert, ready for anything, but she softened enough to answer the questions Jeb asked.

He learned their names, and that they had been on the last escape ship off of Crichton before the catastrophe. Demeter told him their mother promised to find them, but that promise would forever go unfulfilled. She told of her father's promise to return home, another empty promise that would haunt her forever.

Demeter kept that memory of Jeb caring for them close to her heart. The kindness he showed two lost, hungry little girls usually assured her the universe could sometimes provide more than pain and despair.

After that, he kept them around. They helped keep the security quarters clean and got to know everyone on the security team. Jeb found a bunk for them to share and gave them parental care since they had no family.

Jeb was two years into a eight-year contract on the Hephastus. He worked toward a full-time post. Once he accepted a full-time assignment, he promised to take them along if they wanted to join him.

Demeter showed interest in Jeb's security work. As a teenager, she walked his beat with him. Several times, she found herself in a rowdy situation with an unruly passenger. Somehow, she always regained control of the situation.

She understood the security procedures and was adept at tracking and locating something or someone missing. Nothing missing remained missing for long after Demeter absorbed the intel.

Jeb taught her how to keep a calm mind in tense situations. He said her mind was her greatest weapon. He taught her discipline to know when she could think her way out of a situation and when she needed to use forceful means.

The girls attended daily lessons that provided a basic education. Artemis excelled at her more creative endeavors. Demeter was a wiz with numbers and solving any problem given to her.

Demeter denied herself even the slightest of peaceful thoughts at the deluge of cherished memories. She wiped those memories from her mind. Jeb's carelessness and Artemis's disappearance now tainted those sweet remembrances.

Anger simmered within her. Until she discovered what happened to Artemis and had her sister safely returned, all her anger and rage focused on Jeb's incompetence.

How could he just lose contact with her? Why did he ever allow her to leave Pyron?

Technically, Artemis was a grown woman and could do whatever she chose, but to Demeter, she would always be her baby sister.

Still, Jeb had one job to do, and he failed miserably. At the moment, he was no better than her father. What kind of man tells a little girl he loved her, that he would come back for her one day and then never return? All her life, she struggled with her feelings for her father. Sometimes, a great sadness overwhelmed her at the thought of his death in combat. Other times anger overshadowed all else, imagining him abandoning his wife and daughters to run off with a young chippy at his side.

She sighed, realizing she had rubbed her wrist until the flesh was red and irritated. She had to get control of the situation.

It was all about control. She could control capturing a fugitive. Even when the capture did not go according to plan and got messy, she was always in control, or could regain control.

But currently, Jeb did not know where Artemis was. She did not know where Artemis was. Demeter was not in control of the situation. She hated the fact that she had no control.

The only person in the entire galaxy that she could depend on at the moment was Vesta. She depended on Vesta to be the voice of reason when her anger raged. When she wanted nothing more than to go off and destroy everything, she knew Vesta would be there with a calming, rational voice. They could have entire conversations without saying a word, and sometimes a simple look would suffice. Vesta knew her better than anyone. Better than Demeter knew herself at this point.

Artemis was on Barbera, and then she wasn't. Where did she go? What happened?

Somebody knows.

Footfalls entered the bridge behind her. It could only be Vesta.

The younger woman held a steaming concoction of herbs and vitamins. She called it Tilt and Tilly. Her mother made it for its effect of simultaneously calming nerves while invigorating the mind. Vesta since named it in tribute to her beloved aunts she lost in the Gynoid raid. Aunt Tilt always had a soft, warm voice Vesta found soothing. Aunt Tilly told stories that started her brain racing. She imagined distant planets and astonishing adventures. It was how she preferred remembering them.

Taking her seat, Vesta pushed Demeter's feet off the console and set her mug down. The heavy boot heels rattled the metal grid work underfoot with a thud.

"Any luck tracking my sister's beacon?" Demeter asked. She watched the steam shimmer atop the golden surface of the liquid in the mug.

I wonder if there's any tea left in the kettle.

"No," Vesta said reluctantly. She hated to admit she could not find any life sign of Artemis. "Do you think she removed the implant, that maybe after that thing on Parbola, she doesn't want to be found?"

Demeter brooded at the mere mention of *that thing on Parbola*. It was not her fault. She had enemies throughout the universe.

At least, she believed it was not her fault.

When she could not reach Artemis on Parbola, she naturally assumed the worst. She panicked. How was Demeter supposed to know Artemis was spending a weekend on Parbola with Sandor? She had no clue the girl planned to ask her baby sister's hand in marriage. If she had known, Demeter never would have come crashing in on them like a insane she-demon. She had met Sandor before, briefly, and liked the girl okay, but in that moment of overprotective rage, she did not recognize the orange-haired young woman. Demeter slammed Sandor's skull against the wall when she thought Artemis was in danger.

This altercation led the sisters into a screaming fight, each talking, then screaming over the other with concern for nothing else. Demeter took on the role of the overprotective, overworked parent. Artemis tried to explain to her sister that she was an adult and could make her own decisions.

Occasionally, an item took flight and smashed against a wall.

The screaming stopped only when they realized Sandor was gone. There would be no future wedding for Artemis.

For as horrible as the situation grew, it really escalated when Artemis stormed out in a blind rage, running away from her older sister. She was gone for less than an hour-cycle before Demeter and Vesta tracked her down. Artemis inflicted more damage in that brief span of time than Demeter could have ever imagined possible.

Demeter called in every favor owed her to help rectify Artemis's destruction. When those weren't enough to get Artemis out of trouble, she reluctantly called Jeb. She promised to work a twelve month-cycle tracking contract to repay the new favors incurred to clear Artemis.

It was a nightmare, and the sisters had not seen each other since.

Was that the last time I saw her? She didn't even talk to me when Jeb took her back to Pyron. She didn't even look back at me. That was years ago!

Demeter swallowed down the bitter memory. Artemis would never forgive her for all the resentment and fury she caused.

Forgiveness was a privilege she would worry about once she knew her sister was safe.

"I think she's somewhere where the signal can't reach us," Demeter said.

"Roger that." Vesta tapped a lighted button on the console, followed by a long sip of her Tilt and Tilly.

"Let me know when we reach the Barbera system." Demeter stood and stretched her tired body. She could not remember the last time she slept for more than a quick nap.

"That would be now," the pilot said, eyes glued to the vidscreen.

Flexing her fingers and then popping her back, Demeter said, "Good. Let's land and find someone to answer our questions."

Chapter 7:
Mayhem in the Marketplace

The Barbera marketplace was congested with bodies from all over the galaxy. Demeter pushed forward, leading Vesta. The pilot suffered from wandering eyes and a constant desire to shop. She wanted to visit several carts and kiosks.

Everything was available for purchase, for a price. Excited voices filled the air, bartering and negotiating. Vesta noted every offering from the surrounding vendors. One sold factory-made parts for every model of spacecraft imaginable. Another sold computer components and tech gear. Others peddled exotic fruits and vegetables and garments of fine linens.

Some merchants sold contraband. In abundance, illegal black-market copies of video-plays on vid-screen cassette tapes. More to her interest were the vendors offering ancient bound texts. Written on actual paper from such prophets as Asimov, Bradbury, Clarke, and Heinlein, her eyes widened with delight scanning the spines.

If not for Demeter's mission, Vesta would check out the titles. She was sure she already read most of them on a vid-screen reader via the Wolfhound's vid-archives. They were among the most precious items in the marketplace.

Deemed forbidden, governing bodies throughout the galaxy

outlawed the texts. Their chief claim was they wasted natural resources. They never considered the synthetic alternatives used by governments and industries. They wasted reams of paper-like material recording their treaties, constitutions, regulations, and negotiations.

The bound texts were a rare treat for anyone who enjoyed holding a text in their hands and reading the printed words off the paper. Many people hated touching them, let alone actually reading them. To some, they did not seem natural. It was too foreign compared to reading off a vid-screen reader.

"Busy here today," Demeter said. She observed the various species in all their unique styles of dress milling about. Some haggled in tongues she was unfamiliar with. That always startled her because she thought she had met every species inhabiting the universe.

A blue-skinned Arborian, his horned forehead adorned with jewels and shiny symbols of his culture, approached Vesta. He noticed her inspecting his fruit cart and offered her what looked like a plump purple apple. She smiled and shook her head politely and continued following Demeter. The Arborian shrugged his huge shoulders and looked to attract the next shopper to his fruit cart.

"This is going to be like finding a fleck of dust in an asteroid belt," Vesta said. She dodged another kiosk that caught her eye. The vendor displayed a shimmering square of fabric. She could easily fold and twist it into a cute top that would look absolutely amazing against her light complexion. Realizing she stopped moving, she skipped a step to catch up with Demeter, who did not slow down.

"Let's go," Demeter said whenever she noticed Vesta lagging.

A figure swathed in a flowing, threadbare cloak and hood watched their every movement. When they passed, the figure followed at a close but inconspicuous distance, blending into the crowd.

They were easy to follow. Demeter was tall enough to spot and no one else quite had the same color of hair. The smaller one, the pilot, kept dawdling to inspect merchandise, which constantly hindered his tracking.

The cloaked figure studied the surroundings to ensure no one was becoming wise to his actions. He continued his pursuit; sure no one was watching.

When the figure's attention turned back to his prey, they were gone.

Gone!

It was impossible.

Then the younger woman straightened upright near a kiosk of glassware. The warrior Demeter was gone.

The figure sighed and pursued the younger woman. When the distance between them was close enough to reach out and grab her, there was a gentle tapping on his shoulder.

Demeter appeared behind the figure. Her laser pistol drawn; she pressed the muzzle into his hooded skull.

"Go ahead. Lay a hand on her. I dare you."

Demeter directed the figure toward the nearest wall, out of the way of the unending flow of milling bodies. Vesta also brandished her sidearm.

"I mean you no harm." The voice was old and gnarled. There was nothing threatening about the tone.

Demeter lowered her pistol. She yanked the hood from the figure's head, revealing the terrified old humanoid underneath. His eyes widened with fear. His crusty lower lip wavered with uncertain dread of what might happen next. Beneath the cloak, he was a trembling bag of bones.

The guy looks familiar.

His attempt at smiling came across as ghastly.

A scar divided his weathered face like an inflamed bolt of lightning. They noticed he could not stand straight. A large hunch forced a crook in his back.

"I know you," Demeter said, recognizing the humanoid at last. "Didn't I bring you in one time?"

He offered a rotten smile. "Yes, yes. Sonyx is my name. You claimed a bounty on me once for skipping bail. I have made good on my incarceration. I am fully reformed."

Demeter doubted the humanoid's claim of reformation, but she played along.

"Well then, why were you following us? Why did you make a move on Vesta?"

"No, no. You misunderstand. I approach you as an ally. Information about your sister. I have some." The smile simmering on his weathered lips gave him a menacing appearance, but he was harmless. Demeter leaned toward him.

"You know where my sister is? Spit it out or you'll be spitting out your teeth." Demeter tensed.

The smile was gone, and he put his frail hands up in surrender. "Please, no hostile. I'll tell. I'll tell. Here, here."

He gestured for them to follow him into the shadows of a side street. Both women were on alert and Vesta scanned the immediate area to identify anything that might suggest there was an ambush awaiting them. No one in the marketplace paid them any attention.

"Why so secretive? What are you afraid of?" Vesta asked. Sonyx stopped his shuffling gait halfway down the side street and put a wrinkled hand on the nearby wall to steady himself. He turned to face the women.

"The law here is not honorable. Bad people." He was of breath.

"Crooked lawmen?" Demeter said. "What does that have to do with my sister?"

"They arrested her," Sonyx said. His words blew out of his dry throat like a windstorm. "Police took her away, flying." He looked toward the sky, wiggling wrinkled fingers for emphasis.

"Arrested? Why would they arrest her?" Demeter asked. Her tone demanded a reasonable explanation.

Sonyx only shook his head.

Vesta spoke. "Do you know where they took her?"

"Not sure. Off-world definitely."

"What else do you know?" It took all Demeter's restraint not to grab the old humanoid and shake the information out of him.

"Six sun rises ago. It happened. Her arrest. In the town square. At night." He looked physically drained.

"That's it?" Vesta asked. She tried to sound hard, but she felt sympathy for the pathetic old humanoid.

"That's all I know," he said. "Thank you. Please." He slightly bowed to the women.

"All right. Get out of here," Demeter said. She dismissed him.

"Reward for ally?" he asked. His words meek, his smile appearing grotesque, no matter how it formed on his face. "I told you good."

Demeter leaned into him until he backed away, and his head bumped the wall behind him.

"Your reward is getting to walk away."

She turned and strode back into the bustling street.

When Demeter was far enough away, Vesta pushed a coin into his withered palm.

"Get going," Vesta whispered, then caught up with Demeter.

Sonyx shuffled off to the other end of the side street, looked both ways, and then disappeared into the shadows. Demeter and Vesta continued searching the market.

"Well, that's something," Vesta said.

"Not much."

"But something," the younger woman said. "The question is, why would lawmen pick up your sister? Drunk and disorderly?"

"Not like her." At least, at one time, it would not have been like her. Demeter hated to admit that she could not say for sure if that was true now. Was it possible that Artemis had become a party girl? Anything could have happened since the last time the sisters saw one another. The thought did not make her happy.

"I know, but Parbola…" Vesta's voice trailed off, swallowed up in the ruckus of the surrounding crowd.

"Forget Parbola," Demeter snapped. "Something shady is going on. She disappeared six sunrises ago. We need to find out more."

"What's our next move?"

"We need intel straight from the horse's ass." Demeter smiled.

There was a tug in the pit of Vesta's stomach. She sensed a plan formulating.

"From the law? How?"

"You know," Demeter said. A wild gleam sparkled in her eyes.

"Oh, no. You're not serious, are you?"

"You bet I am."

There was no point arguing, fighting, or trying to convince Demeter of any other course of action. The gleam sparkling in her eyes let Vesta know a plan of action was about to be set in motion. Vesta accepted her role as damage control agent. Her job was to ensure Demeter caused the bare minimum of collateral damage.

Vesta surveyed the marketplace. She noticed a big tough alien and his friend exiting a side street. They approached a fruit vendor's cart. It was the blue skinned Arborian who earlier offered her the purple apple.

Pirates, they were Draconians, a good foot and a half taller than Demeter. Each outweighed the women's combined weight. Throughout the galaxy, Draconians took what they wanted. The fruit vendor's wares were like anything else. The bigger of the two picked up a piece of fruit, took a large bite, and set it back down on the cart. His friend laughed.

Protesting, the Arborian merchant demanded payment for the fruit, and both Draconians laughed. When the merchant persisted, the first Draconian shoved him into his cart. The wheels broke free of their chocks and the cart rolled backwards into another vendor cart. The Arborian splayed across his cart as fruit spilled onto the street.

"That one?" Vesta asked with a wicked smile. She looked like a little girl discovering a wonderful new toy.

"That one," Demeter agreed. She returned the smile.

Vesta nodded.

Shike, the Draconian that shoved the merchant, swiped another purple apple from the street. He squeezed it to a pulp in his huge hand. His partner, Mayne, laughed. The merchant scrambled to his feet and tried to collect the fruit, still rolling about the feet of the crowd. No one stopped to help. No one wanted to get involved.

"Hey, big fella," Demeter called over to Shike. The Draconian wiped his hand on his vest and turned to face her.

"I think the vendor would like for you to pay for all that."

"What's it to you?" Shike hissed.

"I don't like thieves." Her hands tightened into fists. Her leg muscles flexed, waiting for the command to spring to action.

"Are you calling me a thief?" The amusement was gone from his voice. He stepped toward Demeter. When he inhaled a deep intake of breath, his body appeared to double.

Vesta stepped between her partner and Shike.

"I heard it. You called him a thief," Vesta said. "This guy is too stupid to understand. His friend too."

Mayne, who enjoyed watching his friend torment the merchant, now took a stance next to Shike. The Draconians sized up the women. They seemed so tiny and delicate, so easy to break.

Galaxy Warriors

"You gonna take this from a pair of frails, Shike?" Mayne asked.

Demeter knew *frails* was the word Draconians used for anyone they felt weaker than them. It was their word for women. The word always pissed her off when she heard it.

"Nothing frail about us, crater-face." If they were at all unsure of her intentions before, her tone made everything clear.

"You feel froggy, boys?" Demeter asked. She teased them with a half-smile. "Then jump."

"That does it!" Without warning, Shike shot a fist out with shocking speed.

Demeter ducked within an inch of his swing. Had the giant fist connected, her skull would be a jigsaw puzzle, the pieces scattered across the street like the Arborian vendor's fruit.

For such big boys, they commanded unbelievable swiftness. Mayne flicked out a laser knife. The blade sizzled to electric life and was as ugly as either of the two Draconians. The eight-inch laser blade buzzed in the air. Mayne flicked it from one paw to the other.

Determined to make the first move, Vesta stomped Mayne's foot with the heel of her boot. She put all her weight on it and caught the big creep by surprise. An expert blow to his wrist sent the laser blade spinning harmlessly under a nearby cart.

The crowd watched the fracas. It was hard not to notice two women engaged in hand-to-hand combat with the giant Draconians. If most didn't stop to watch the brawl, they slowed to observe what was unfolding. The wave of people moved around them like a flowing stream to avoid the combatants.

Demeter vaulted herself over a vendor's table of industrial tools like Zorn steamers and laser clippers of all sizes. Shike barely missed grabbing her by her trailing hair. He lunged forward. When he did, Demeter pulled the canopy top shading the table down, covering him. Blind and vulnerable to attack, Shike bellowed in outrage. Demeter seized the opportunity to slam a couple of quick jabs into the side of his thick skull.

Mayne punched Vesta in the face with a solid blow. Vesta at once retaliated with a series of quick, forceful jabs to his midsection, a weak point for Draconians. He grabbed his stomach protectively and

Vesta spun, sending a roundhouse kick against his skull. Mayne dropped.

Scared for everyone's safety, a nearby vendor beckoned the local lawmen. The spectators in the crowd cheered the fighters as the battle raged. Two pint-sized Griglings, lizard people, mimicked the actions of the fighters on the sidelines. The lawmen arrived just in time to see Vesta drop Mayne with the roundhouse kick and Demeter squeezing the breath out of Shike. She held him in a fierce headlock. The Draconian gasped for breath.

Four lawmen surrounded the two women, their laser weapons drawn.

"Stop your unruly activity at once." The lead lawman was itching for some trigger action. "Put your hands above your heads."

Demeter studied them. She knew they hoped for any excuse to vaporize them into piles of smoking bones. She responded by shoving Shike's unconscious body toward them. The lawmen moved in tighter.

"I repeat. Stop your unruly activity at once and put your hands above your head."

Demeter could not tell them apart. They looked and sounded the same. She suspected they all crawled out of the same test tube together. She shared a quick glance with Vesta. The younger woman responded with a knowing wink.

Vesta stomped on the shin of the lawman nearest her and snatched his weapon. Demeter caught another with her elbow and secured his weapon. She fired above their heads.

"Send for the prison transport!" The lead lawman barked into his shoulder radio-comm. "We have two unruly lawbreakers!"

Vesta bludgeoned the officer's forehead with the handle of the laser pistol she snatched. The others jumped on her and wrestled her to the ground. She never stopped fighting them until she heard Demeter's voice.

"Okay, okay. You got us. Take us to the judge."

The struggle ended. A lawman laughed. "I don't know what world you think you're on, chippy." He panted, straining to catch his breath. "There are no judges here. You are going directly to the Prison Planet."

The two lawmen yanked Vesta to her feet. They threw her

against a nearby wall while they secured her wrists in zip cuffs. She worried about what came next.

By comparison, Demeter seemed to welcome the unknown that awaited them. In fact, the prospects of the unknown absolutely delighted her.

Chapter 8:
Welcome to Hell

They spent the first half of their brief journey chained in individual cells. Demeter and Vesta regrouped in the hull with the other prisoners. The hull was identical to the one that transported Artemis to Tartarus a week earlier, but they had no way of knowing that. Cramped, Demeter noticed that none of the arrested women belonged on a prison transport ship.

Demeter felt peace. The shadow of a smile played on her lips. It was weird. Vesta called it the *calm before the storm*. Satisfied with the results of her plan getting them onto Prison Planet, Demeter was ecstatic. One of Demeter's plans might have worked too well.

Two guards patrolled the cell in silent obedience to their captain's orders. The women kept their eyes averted elsewhere. They knew the tiniest whimper could attract enough attention that resulted in a senseless physical reprimand.

The guards have the deadest eyes.

Demeter studied their behavior. Between the lifeless eyes, and the way they acted, like robots, she knew it was Kapitron injections. Dr. Kraspin devised the compound. His nickname, Doctor of Death, reverberated throughout the galaxy. The name came from his penchant for creating more pain in his patients than his willingness to ease their suffering.

Kapitron was the chemical compound he created while researching a treatment to ease the mind-shakes. The veterans of the psychic wars experienced horrendous mind-shakes a short time after their tours of duty ended. The PSY-soldiers were a rare breed. Their chromosomal structure was highly unique. The doctor experimented on them with great delight.

Endless experimentations proved Kapitron did nothing to ease the mind-shakes. However, to his surprise, it rendered the subjects completely susceptible to his command. They performed his every command, but only to a certain degree.

At the end of the experiments, Kapitron proved to create a perfect soldier. Unfortunately, the veterans he used as his original test subjects were too weak for the compound to perform properly. Those test subjects failed. They perished, the mind-shakes magnifying and causing excruciating agony until death was the only cure. At that point, Dr. Kraspin was extremely eager to ease their suffering.

When he had no more PSY-soldiers, he turned to more suitable subjects. Unsanctioned factions within the Star League provided Dr. Kraspin with ground soldiers as test subjects for results.

Kraspin's tests on the inexperienced, younger soldiers proved successful.

Kapitron's use in various branches of the Star League, and throughout the galaxy for law keeping, gained immediate acceptance. The Space Service refused to endorse the mind-altering drug. Leaders in the Star League, however, found the drug useful. An army populated with soldiers incapable of questioning commands and feeling no fear were perfect soldiers. Soldiers on Kapitron followed commands to the letter. They performed at the highest level of excellence, without fear or empathy clouding their sense of duty.

The guards on Prison Planet made for perfect recipients of Dr. Kraspin's Kapitron injections. They were unthinking, obedient zombies in guard uniforms.

Demeter overheard one young woman, Bekah, talking to another. In hushed whispers, she told how the lawmen barged into the home of her parents demanding tax payments they knew nothing about. When the young woman tried defending her parents, who were weary from working in the Temple Mithra ice fields all day, they arrested her for being unruly.

"They arrested you because you're a woman," Lucretia hissed under her breath, just loud enough for a guard to hear. The guard shoved her to the floor and warned her to be quiet.

"Hey!" Demeter snapped at the guard; the calm smile gone. Her eyes dared him to raise a hand at her. She'd have those emotionless eyes shoved down his throat if he tried anything. He recognized something in her steely gaze that served as a warning. His attention diverted to a woman moving nervously, bouncing from one foot to the other. He growled at her to stay still.

"This isn't too bad," Vesta whispered, mostly to herself. The sarcasm was extra spicy. "It could be worse."

"Sure," Demeter said. "It'll be fine."

A prisoner nearby snorted a laugh. Demeter focused on her. She was a stout fighter with a mane of green hair. It was colorant, not natural. It gave the woman an eerie resemblance to the ancient Gorgon; the mythical creature with serpents for hair that transformed men into stone with just one glance.

Rastia watched Vesta, overhearing the pilot's whisper. Among all the women in the transport cell, the green-haired witch definitely looked like she belonged here.

"First time?" she said to Vesta.

"What?" Vesta looked up. Rastia glared at her.

"First time on a prison ship?" The witch woman cackled.

"Why?" Vesta asked.

The woman smiled. Her teeth were a shade darker than the green dye coloring her hair. "Wait till we hit atmo."

Demeter didn't recognize the term.

Vesta leaned toward Demeter and said quietly, "Atmosphere." Demeter nodded. She turned back to the woman.

"We've hit atmo before. It will be fine," Demeter said, her tone flip.

As if to contradict Demeter's confidence, the transport ship rumbled violently. It shook, tossing its living cargo carelessly about. The women gasped and held on to each other. Demeter assumed whoever was piloting the transport was also taking Kapitron and didn't care about their safety.

Vesta watched through a portal window. Bursts of flame scorched the exterior glass. She felt the heat and backed away.

Darkness gave way to brilliant bolts of brightness.

"We're hitting too fast," Vesta said. A guard warned her to be quiet.

"Told ya. Atmo!" Rastia snorted another laugh.

The transport ship continued its furious shaking through re-entry. Bodies flung about. Demeter's stomach flopped. The surrounding prisoners pushed into her. She fought to keep her balance. Rastia's snorting turned into a demented cackle.

When Demeter feared she could no longer hold her stomach, the shaking ceased. A bright blue, overly sunny sky peered through all the portals and the transport ship leveled off.

Rastia continued her cackling well after the guards warned her to stop. They could not reach her among all the scattered bodies. What did it matter, anyway? They would brutalize her soon enough.

"Welcome to Prison Planet." The green-haired woman said. She laughed. The transport landed with a clanking thud.

"Also known as hell," she said. The portal hatch hissed open. Brilliant, hot sunlight filled the hull.

Chapter 9:
Enyo and the New Warrior

After the transport vessel set down, dead-eyed guards herded the prisoners off the ship in a single file line. The burning sands of Tartarus, Prison Planet, greeted them.

Demeter surveyed the desolation surrounding them. Tartarus offered a vast sea of sand and heat waves, and nothing more. The ugly prison lay ahead. It was the only structure populating the bleak landscape. The planet was a burned-out wasteland.

There was nowhere to escape. The entire planet was a prison.

Memorizing every minor detail, Demeter noted that the name on the prison transport ship they exited was the Cygnus. The letters stood out in large block letters on the ship's starboard side. The ship docked next to the Cygnus was the Palomino.

"Move!" A guard shoved her hard enough for her to lose her balance. She fell to one knee.

"Oh, no," Vesta whispered. The young pilot became ill.

A smile appeared on Demeter's face. She raised her head and looked at the guard, one brow arched.

"Get back in line and keep moving for prison processing." Cletus grabbed the laser pistol at his side for emphasis.

Galaxy Warriors

Please don't act like a deranged person, Demeter. Please don't get us blasted here.

Vesta tensed, hoping to communicate those words to her partner telepathically. She was not of the Nestor race of natural telepaths, nor one of the old PSY-soldiers. She knew it would do no good, anyway.

"I said get back in line." Cletus towered over her. She rose to her feet. Everyone watched, stunned silent. For Vesta, it was like waiting for a deadly Yanti serpent to strike.

With one fluid sweep, Demeter took the guard's legs out from under him and stomped a boot on the center of his chest. The breath blasted out of his lungs.

The other guards were on her, laser pistols ready.

She threw up her hands in a lazy forfeit and returned to the line formation. She could not resist the smug smile that her lips formed.

"What are you?" Cletus asked. Another guard helped him up. His chest hurt, like a scrambler just rolled over him. He struggled to regain his breath.

"What do you think I am, you scrawny creep?" She said it loud enough for the benefit of everyone in line. "I am a woman."

Enyo, the warden, peered from the watchtower as the new prisoners marched off the transport ship. Her cyber-eye focused on them, making note of each new prisoner as they trod onto the sand. Her electronic left eye resembled the lens of a picture recording device. A skull harness similar to an eyepatch secured the bionic eye in place. The cyber-eye whirled and clicked, focusing from one prisoner to the next.

At one time, Enyo had been quite beautiful. There were even those who still thought her beautiful. Tall, her figure was supple and desirable, and her long brunette hair framed her fine facial features. Her good eye sparkled when it caught the light just right. She puffed smoke around the cigar between her lips and sloshed the ice chips in the tumbler of scotch with her robotic right hand. The cyber-eye continued scanning each fresh face.

"The new group, Warden Enyo," Zorn said. He sat at the watchtower's security console viewing the incoming prisoners on a large vid-screen. Warden Enyo never called him by his name. She sneered at him. His eyes were not dead and emotionless like the guards. Long ago he learned to adopt their basic disinterest in meeting the warden's gaze or questioning her orders.

"I see," she said absently, continuing to click the ice chips against the tumbler.

"They look unruly," Zorn said with great distaste. He pressed buttons on the console. A sequence of colored buttons zoomed the security camera closer to the new inmates.

"They always do." She turned from the window and drank down the last of the scotch in one quick swallow.

She clanked the tumbler down on the console next to Zorn. The tech was motionless. Shocked, he watched an altercation between Cletus and a tall, red-haired prisoner.

"What is this?" the warden said. She watched the vid-screen with mounting curiosity.

Enyo studied the woman's quick moves, her confidence and obvious disregard for authority. Her interest in this new prisoner grew when the prisoner swiftly, in one fluid motion, swept the guard's legs out from under him. Shock froze the other prisoners where they stood. The other guards reacted. Something made Warden Enyo believe the guards were insufficient to tame this new prisoner.

She continued watching with great interest.

Never had she seen any of her guards taken down before by a woman. Even with laser pistols drawn, she could see the auburn haired prisoner was completely in charge as the conflict drew to its conclusion.

"What do we have here?" Enyo said. The prisoner's arrest details flashed on the screen. Her cyber-eye processed the scant information it offered. She learned very little about the curious prisoner. There were plans forming for this one.

"Playback the vid-screen cassette recording."

Zorn complied with the command. The tape recording of the security camera footage rolled back to the beginning of the altercation. A cruel smile touched her lips. She watched the altercation again. The redheaded prisoner was a true warrior.

"Should I…" Zorn began, but Enyo cut him off.

"No. Let her pass. I want to see more."

Chapter 10:
Hell Under Multiple Suns

Rex led the incoming prisoners toward the decontamination chamber. His duty guards kept them in line. Moe and Cletus flanked the front of the line. They ensured the women kept moving by shoving them down the hallways towards processing. Tycho and Neander held the rear. They ensured the rest of the women followed.

"Keep moving, vermin. Line up over there." With the coiled whip, Rex motioned toward a long stone wall. Filth covered every surface of the facility. Demeter wondered what the various colored stains splattering the walls were.

Shackles bolted to chains hung high on the wall, just above their heads.

Over a loudspeaker, Warden Enyo's voice boomed. It emitted crackly and tinny sounding.

"Prepare for decontamination."

The women looked at one another. Fear passed from one set of eyes to the next. None of the women dared move.

Vesta looked worried, but Demeter kept cool. The guards began pulling on thick rubber gloves. Two retrieved a coil of hose. Black sludge dripped from the nozzle.

"You heard the warden. Strip down!" Rex's voice echoed down the chamber.

Demeter and Vesta shared a glance. Demeter recognized the horror in her partner's eyes. Vesta looked genuinely terrified.

"Nuh-uh," the pilot said. She was not worried about who would hear her.

"We're here to find Artemis," Demeter said. "We don't want a fight."

Vesta shot her a sarcastic *Oh, really?* glare. Before she could respond, Rastia jumped out of line.

"Prisoners will comply," Rex said.

The stout little green-haired woman spit in Rex's face, cackling with glee.

"Take that pig!" she shrieked. The women in the decontamination chamber cheered her efforts. Unprepared for such an outburst, the guards readied their laser pistols.

"Stand your ground, men," Rex said. The guards raised their weapons.

Moe stepped forward, grabbed at Demeter's poly-armor top and gave it a jerk to rip it free.

"Off with it, chippy!"

It was like a toggle switch flipped inside her.

"I'll tell you what. I'll give you *this*," she said, leaping.

Demeter smashed him in the face. He flailed backwards, arms pinwheeling. The women moved as one, rushing the guards.

Rastia shrieked a war cry and leaped onto Cletus's back. She held tight and rode him like a bucking Dogen. He could not reach her to pull her off and succeeded in only spinning himself dizzy trying to fling her free.

Rex called for more guards. They appeared at once, filling the decontamination chamber.

Where did they come from?

Demeter watched more guards scurry into the chamber. She and Vesta held their own against them when a side door swung open. It banged against the wall with substantial force.

Warden Enyo. A guard tried to keep her from walking into the thick of the ruckus. She pushed him away with enough force to send him spinning backwards like a lost satellite. She strolled into the eye of the storm and approached Vesta.

Enyo considered the pilot for a moment. The cyber-eye clicked.

With reflexes developed in a cyber lab, Enyo locked her robotic hand around Vesta's throat and lifted. The young pilot suddenly dangled inches from the floor. Enyo fired the weapon no one noticed in her other hand. The laser beam sparked off the rock wall above their heads.

Everyone froze, even the guards. Even Rex.

"Enough!" The warden's voice was razor sharp.

Enyo's cyber-eye scanned each prisoner. Digital squares highlighted specific features on each face. At an amazing rate, the cyber-eye collected and analyzed data. Information pertaining to each woman appeared beside the image. One after the other, past the green-haired witch that started the ruckus to Demeter, where she stopped.

"Stand down right now and prepare for decontamination," Enyo said.

Vesta grabbed at the unfeeling metal hand choking her. Her toes tried locating the floor below her.

"Or?" Demeter challenged.

"Or…" the warden drew out her words slowly. "First, I'll gas all of you. Then, when you're flapping on the floor gasping for air, I'll slit your throats. Got it?"

Demeter motioned to the other prisoners to stand down. The ones clutching the guards released them. Once the guards were free, the prisoners backed away. All eyes watched the warrior and the warden.

"Yeah, we got it. Now release her."

Vesta's face turned blue.

"You don't give the orders here." Enyo raised Vesta another inch.

Demeter's steely eyed gaze dropped. Biting the inside of her mouth, she said, "Release her. Please."

Vesta dropped to the floor, gasping for air. Demeter was at her side. She helped her up and backed her away from Enyo, keeping her body between her partner and the sadistic warden.

Enyo focused on the rest of the women. The cyber-eye identified each prisoner, searching for the one with the green hair.

"You," she said, finding Rastia.

Before the woman responded with further insolence, Enyo's laser pistol fired. The green-haired woman froze, suspended just above the chamber's floor by a bolt of red laser light until she collapsed into a charred pile of bones.

"Listen up, chippies." Enyo strolled down the line of prisoners so she could make her point clear. The greasy smell of charred flesh permeated the air.

"I am the law here. I am the one in charge. You do as you are told and maybe life will be… bearable. But, if you cause me or my guards any grief…" Her voice trailed off, stopping to gaze at Demeter. Her cyber-eye whirled and focused on the prisoner warrior.

"Well, there are worse things here than a ray blast through the brain."

Enyo turned on her heels and exited the chamber. Her flowing emerald cloak billowed behind her.

The guards lined the women in a row. Rex gave the command to douse them in the viscous, syrupy decontamination chemical. It neutralized foreign substances on their bodies before entering lock-up. It also immunized them from any of the planet's foreign microbes they may be vulnerable to.

Although drugged and emotionless, the guards seemed to relish dousing the women in the chemical sludge. Their eyes never came alive, but their sadistic joy was obvious. Especially Cletus and the one named Tycho. They were unnecessarily cruel when they got to Demeter and Vesta. The black blast doused each woman, drowning them in its sickening chemical scent.

Afterwards, wet clothes clinging to their bodies, the black chemical dripping from every part of them, the guards forced the women to strip. The dead-eyed guards hosed them again for "good measure," per their captain.

Demeter gritted her teeth while the cold spray pounded her naked body.

All of you will pay.

The thought was of little comfort as the cold chemical wash blasted the bounty hunter a second time.

When the women marched to their cellblock in a single file line, they were mostly dry, except for their hair. They wore dry prison garb, which was little more than rags stitched into crude gowns. The gowns covered more or less, depending on who wore them. Because of her height, Demeter's gown barely covered her. Forget how emotionless the guards appeared. She felt their dirty eyes on her exposed midriff and legs.

A guard prodded both Demeter and Vesta along.

"I'm going. I'm going." Demeter held her hands where they were visible. She fought the desire to make fists.

Prisoners milled through the humongous cellblock. Many clustered in groups. Loners wandered the perimeter of the containment bars. Eyes watched the world beyond the bars, their minds a million light years away.

A cluster of inmates surrounded a black-haired woman. Scars and tattoos, some intertwining, covered her flesh. She exuded an aura of menace. She was dangerous the same way a laser knife was dangerous, dangling precariously overhead on a frayed string. The other prisoners showed her the utmost respect.

A quiet fell over the cellblock when the new inmates entered. Flipping her black hair to one side, Circe studied each new prisoner. Everyone sized them up.

Chrona, a smaller, more excitable woman, stood by Circe's side. She whispered something into Circe's ear. The tattooed woman nodded.

Demeter locked eyes with Circe.

"Well, we're here now. What's the plan?" Unsure how it could be any worse, Vesta noticed the holes cut into the dirty concrete floor in one corner of the cell. The lavatory.

"I'm working on it," Demeter said. Her eyes never diverted from Circe.

Circe, flanked by Chrona on her left and Dhyana and Halla on her right, strolled toward them.

"Is that Circe?" Surprise and disbelief colored Vesta's expression.

Demeter did not answer. She continued tracking Circe's every movement.

"We haven't seen her since…"

"I killed her husband and sent her to prison," Demeter said, finishing the thought. Her muscles tightened. She was alert and connected to the immediate area around her.

"On Tolo 4. What's she doing here?"

"I don't know." Demeter watched. Circe strolled closer.

Circe moved within striking distance of Demeter, and the women in the area scattered. Dhyana and Halla grabbed Vesta. They dragged her away, slamming her against the cell bars. Pain ran up her spine. She groaned. Chrona called out. Demeter barely understood the Akiran language.

They circled each other like Galaxina panthers. Their eyes locked on one another. The tension between the two warriors swelled. The atmosphere within the cell grew thick.

Circe smiled. The metal shiv in one hand caught the light, gleamed.

"Surprised to see me, bounty hunter?"

Zorn's tinny voice echoed over the PA system before either warrior made a move.

"Stand down, Circe."

"Not a chance." She waved the deadly shiv. She planned to bury it deep into Demeter's throat.

The PA crackled again. Zorn's voice boomed. "Stand down or suffer the consequences."

His finger hovered over a blinking red button on the console. He knew the protocol. You did not want to risk being the one to not act fast enough in the initial moments of an inmate confrontation. Inmate confrontations had their place, but the cellblock was not that place.

Circe held a moment longer before breaking eye contact. She laughed, turning to walk away. Her entourage followed. The shiv changed hands and vanished.

"Later gator meat," she said. Then she vanished like the shiv.

Demeter exhaled. She was tense, geared up and ready for anything.

"Must be some consequence," Vesta said.

Zorn's voice echoed again, less abrasive but just as harsh.

"Lights out in ten, chippies. You'll need your rest for your full day of penal service tomorrow." The PA popped loudly with feedback, then died.

"Did he just say…"

"Never mind," Demeter said. "Come on."

After a quick search, they located their vacant bunks. Numbers printed on mattresses matched the identification number assigned to them in processing. It was the same number stitched onto the backs of the gowns.

They crawled onto the dirty mattresses. Vesta fluffed her pillow and covered herself with the paper-thin blanket. She let out a sigh, which she often did after a long day.

"Cozy," she said in a little girl's voice.

"We've camped worse," Demeter said.

"I doubt you have a plan." Vesta's eyes closed. A forced smile appeared on her face.

Demeter ignored the comment. "If we're going to find Artemis, we first need to get a lay of the land."

She's stalling me, Vesta thought. *I know she is. Her plan began and ended with getting us arrested and dumped on this rock. Now she's just making it up as she went along.*

Vesta wiggled on the lumpy mattress, trying to get comfortable. When she settled in, she said, "Yeah, okay."

"Tomorrow we'll look around and see what we can sniff out."

A nearby inmate started snoring. Then another, and more.

"I hope it smells better than this place," Vesta whispered, so as not to awaken her cellmates.

"What's the worry? You're decontaminated."

A metallic clatter rumbled throughout the vast cellblock. The outer sun shields lowered on worn gears, covering windows and skylights. Prison Planet, with its multiple suns, never grew dark. The metal shielding blocked out the forever day so prisoners could get eight hours of sleep.

Once darkness swallowed the cellblock, the dim glow of scattered red night lights flickered to life.

In the darkness, Zorn's staticky voice called out, "Shut up and go to sleep!"

Demeter glanced over at Vesta. Her partner had done just that. Vesta was asleep. The gentle sound of steady breathing drifted from her bunk.

"Goodnight, partner," Demeter said.

Long ago, Demeter had learned to relax her body and brain to fall into a quick, restful sleep. Her brain was still on alert, and she could wake up ready for action, but she soon joined in the calliope of snoring, slumbering prisoners.

Chapter 11:
Midnight Visits

"Demeter, you must find your sister!"

The words of an old man. His voice sounded tired. Demeter did not know who he was. She had never seen him before in her life. At least she didn't think she had seen him before.

They were high on a cliff overlooking an ocean of crystal blue water. She had only seen such a place on vid-screen tapes. A cool wind blew through her hair. It felt like gentle fingers caressing her.

Wherever it was, it was the most peaceful place she had ever experienced.

She felt such inner peace and tranquility. Demeter basked in the serenity, not worrying where she was.

"Find Artemis," the old man repeated. His words were fragile, but urgent.

"Who are you?" she asked. He looked familiar, but she was sure she did not know him. He seemed harmless, even friendly. It was just her instinct.

Relaxed, she felt vulnerable to the world around her, but she was not concerned. It was the oddest sensation not to be on full alert. She felt like she was floating in the crisp air. He was so close she could touch him.

She reached for him, but he was gone. He watched her from the top of a distant hillock. Colors crisscrossed the sky behind him, orange and yellow. The ocean was gone from view. She heard crashing waves behind her, smelled the sweet water.

Despite the distance between them, his voice came to her as clearly as if he were standing next to her. He repeated himself.

"I'm trying to find her," she said. She grew defensive. "That's why I came to Prison Planet."

"Find Artemis." An old woman's voice soft in her ears. She appeared beside her. She brushed Demeter's hand, and her touch was comforting. It sent little bolts of electricity up her arm, which made the tiny hairs stand on end. Her touch was familiar.

Are you...

The old woman repeated her words. They filled Demeter's head.

"Find your sister, Demeter."

Demeter closed her eyes. Another breeze caressed her face. On a distant hillock, the old woman stood next to the old man.

"Now wake up!" they said. Their voices boomed like a warning signal.

Demeter snapped awake bathed in the red glow of the night lights. The point of the shiv pressed into her chin. She was on full alert.

Circe stared at her; her face framed by her dark hair. She gave the shiv a little flick, and Demeter felt it against her throat. She swallowed.

"Not so tough now, are you, bounty hunter?" The words dripped with menace.

"What do you want?" It came out a dry choke. Demeter felt her body tense and awaited the tip of the shiv to puncture her flesh.

"It's not what I want, it's what I owe," Circe said. The red glow of the night lights highlighted her features. She was a demon walking among women.

Demeter dared not look away. She sensed Circe's flunkies were nearby. The two from earlier no doubt held Vesta down, keeping her from helping. She imagined how scared her partner must be, unable to help.

"I owe you the sight of your own blood. Do you understand?" Circe looked deep into Demeter's eyes for a long moment.

Circe drove the point of the makeshift blade in just enough to draw a bead of blood.

Focused on her midnight assailant, the warrior did not so much as wince, the slight prick blocked out. She learned long ago to ignore the pain. Circe held the blade so Demeter could watch the crimson drop run down its length.

"That's good," Circe said. She observed all the sleeping prisoners around them. No one stirred. She looked back down at Demeter.

"Crazy thing about this place. New gator meat riles up the old gator meat. And your arrival has really got them going."

"I am not your enemy," Demeter said. She watched the shiv for any quick movements.

"Oh, I know. I don't even blame you for the death of Nadoo. I probably would have killed him myself before long, the stupid sod."

"Then why…"

Circe cut her off. She pressed the shiv, like a finger, to Demeter's lips.

"I have it good here. I have a posse and I have respect. And I'm not letting you mess it up."

The shiv disappeared. Demeter detected the slight rustle of metal on flesh. It changed hands until it was gone. Circe leaned closer until Demeter felt the woman's breath on her cheek.

"Tomorrow in the Fight Zone, I will cut out your heart and eat it to defend my title."

Fight Zone?

Wait… what Fight Zone?

Demeter did not understand.

Circe patted Demeter's cheek and smiled.

"So, nighty-night, bounty hunter. Rest up for your one and only performance tomorrow. The spectators are going to love you."

Circe slipped away in the darkness. Demeter rubbed the nick on her throat. Circe's last words haunted her. *Tomorrow in the Fight Zone, I will cut out your heart and eat it to defend my title.* What was she talking about? What title?

It was then Demeter noticed Vesta. The pilot was breathing steadily, sleeping soundly, and oblivious to the midnight assault.

So much for restraining her during my attack, Demeter thought sourly. *How could anyone sleep in this place?*

Demeter laid back, unable to drift back to sleep. Her mind raced with images of whatever the Fight Zone was.

The night passed. The rattle of the sun shields rising filled the cellblock. Sunlight thundered throughout the structure. Demeter had long forgotten Circe's words and wondered only about that beautiful place in her dream. It was not a familiar planet.

She could not shake the feeling she somehow knew the old people.

Chapter 12:
Flight from the Fight Zone

The transport doors swung open. Bright light from multiple suns vanquished the darkness inside the carrier. Demeter was on high alert, her body and mind primed for anything.

"Move!" Rex said. His voice roared. The captain of the guards seemed fiercer today. He did not wear his helmet or mask. The multiple suns baked his perfectly smooth head. His bark was all the women needed to hear to exit the carrier hurriedly.

The landscape was vast, desolate in all directions. It was mostly flat except for the occasional jut of rocks scattered about. Prickly trees twisted upward in odd shapes. They resembled skeletal hands clawing out of a grave. Lying awake the night before, Demeter pictured some kind of coliseum, or arena, not an open wasteland.

"Where's the fence?" Demeter wasn't asking anyone in particular. There should at least be a fence to keep combatants corralled during the bouts.

Where did the spectators sit? Circe mentioned spectators.

Am I missing something?

The women lined up outside the scrambler. Tired gears sprang to life, their groaning filled the air. A giant vid-screen rose from the sandy surface. The screen stretched high into the blue sky and, when exposed in its entirety, locked into place with a sharp hydraulic hiss.

A giant number five flashed across the vid-screen with an audible pop. The number four quickly followed. The screen popped; a number three appeared. Another pop and the number two. Static blazoned across the screen's surface. It went blank with one last pop and came instantly to life. A grand dais appeared. Spectators milled about the rows of plush seating, settling in for the day's amusements. Excitement colored their expectant faces.

The spectators were wealthy, people of power. They did not fight wars; they instigated and profited from war. To them, war was a recreational pastime, an opportunity to make another quick billion Mega-credit.

There was no telling what clandestine theater the spectators broadcast from. Demeter knew everything about Enyo's little Friday night fights was illegal. The brazen commission of such crimes on the penal planet shocked her.

The warden's scrambler zoomed toward the screen in a cloud of dust. It approached from the opposite end of the Fight Zone, just beyond the erected vid-screen. Enyo stepped out and greeted the spectators with a gracious bow and sweep of her cape.

From the cargo bay of the scrambler, Zorn opened a crate full of video-drones. He activated them. Each video-drone took flight with a whirling buzz. They bounced in the air overhead and began broadcasting to the spectators on the dais. A cheer rumbled from the crowd.

Another scrambler with a giant covered cargo cage pulled up. It neared the prisoner transport scrambler. Enyo took center stage before her audience.

"Ladies and gentlemen, Lords and Ladies," Enyo said. She raised her arms in a welcoming gesture. Her cyber-eye locked on one regal female spectator on the giant screen. She smiled and bowed respectfully. "Your Eminence."

The dignitary, a slightly older woman with blond hair twisted to one side, returned the gesture. Polished jewels sparkled in her hair, and she wore a flowing gown of azure and silver. The spectators roared with enthusiastic anticipation.

"I bid you welcome. I am Enyo, the warden of Prison Planet,

and these are your wager games!"

Another burst of excited applause erupted from the crowd. When the cheers died down, the warden continued.

"The prisoners who will fight today are not bound by chains and they are not bound by fences." She half turned, sweeping her arm across the desolate landscape.

"What stops them from escaping?" It was a voice from the spectators. Other voices joined in, calling out the same question.

Circe, Chrona close by her side, slid next to Demeter. She leaned toward the warrior.

"Listen up, bounty hunter." Demeter turned to meet Circe's gaze; the woman nodded towards the warden.

Continuing her role as ringmaster, Enyo raised her arms higher. "We do not need fences on Prison Planet because there is nowhere to go."

"Has anyone tried to escape?" Vesta asked.

Circe laughed. "Tried? Sure. Succeeded? No."

Circe ran a fingertip down Vesta's bare arm. The pilot shuddered, pulled away.

"Leave her alone, Circe," Demeter warned.

Chrona began muttering. "No chains, no fences. No chains, no fences. No chains, no fences…"

The smaller woman trembled. Her grip on reality slipped away. Her gaze fixed on a point beyond the Fight Zone. A stupor seized her mind, clouding her judgment. She licked her cracked lips. Her eyes focused on a spot far away.

"No, Chrona, I told you. Don't even think about it. There's danger," Circe said.

Chrona's eyes continued peering into the distance. There was nothing out there except open space and the opportunity for escape.

It was obvious what the woman thought. It made Demeter's stomach uneasy. The bounty hunter instinctively expected what happened next.

"No chains! No fences!" Those four words echoed in her head. Chrona became more excited each time she repeated them until she could no longer help herself.

Chrona bolted out of formation.

"No!" Circe went to grab the smaller woman, but Tycho stopped her.

"Back in formation," Tycho said. He struck her in the stomach with the butt of his laser pistol. Air blasted from Circe's lungs. She dropped to her knees, groaning.

Satisfied, the guard fell back to watch the spectacle with the jubilant spectators. They cheered Chrona on her daring escape. The wagering began.

Enyo smiled, watching the wager counter on the comm-tracker she wore on her left wrist. The digital numbers on the tracker's comm-screen rose rapidly. In her head, she calculated the percentage due her just from this one wager game alone.

Chrona sprinted as fast as her little legs would carry her toward the open desert. She ignored the shouts from the guards and her fellow inmates to stop. The crowd of spectators continued cheering her on. She focused only on the rocks and twisted trees and all that glorious open space before her.

She sprinted toward a rock formation. Chrona's mind raced, her stubby legs pumping for all they were worth. If she made it to the rocks, she could gain a vantage point. There may be a cave entrance somewhere in the piled formation. Tunnels ran underneath Prison Planet's surface. Nothing was ever what it seemed. There could even be a cache of weapons stashed within the rocks. So many scenarios played through her mind as she ran.

Circe spit into the sand. She wiped her mouth with the back of her hand. Demeter helped her up.

"Guard's name is Tycho. Rhymes with 'psycho.'" She spit again, her eyes on the guard. Tycho paid her no attention.

"What's going to happen?" Demeter did not want to watch the unfolding madness, but she could not look away.

"You'll see."

Video-drones sprang into action, buzzing through the air to cover the excitement from every angle. The image on the giant vid-screen switched to the multiple points of view the drones offered. Each quarter of the screen covered a unique perspective of the same action. The spectators cheered for more excitement.

Neander approached Enyo.

"A sniper is ready to take her out," he said.

"Belay the order," Enyo said. This was the titillation the spectators expected, even demanded, from the games. It made them happy. It made them wager more. The more they wagered, the bigger percentage of Mega-credits filled her secured account.

Chrona ran further. Although the video-drones stayed on top of her, the spectators became agitated that nothing thrilling happened. This was just a chase.

One moment more. Make them wait for it.

Enyo smiled to herself. She knew how to work the crowd. This was what they desired. The spectacle of life and death. But primarily the death part.

"Warden?"

She turned to Neander and smiled. Her cyber-eye whirled, focusing on the guard.

"Sic the Pharon on her."

"As you wish." Neander hurried off.

"The Pharon!" Enyo said. Her tone triumphant, arms joyously raised. The wild cheers from the crowd filled the field.

No chains! No fences!
No chains! No fences!

These words repeated endlessly in Chrona's mind. She pumped her arms and legs, gasping for breath. A sharp pain stabbed her side. She could not hold up to such physical exertion, but she dared not stop.

Nearly stumbling, she windmilled her arms and maintained her balance. She kept moving. The video-drones chased her, and the crowd roared. But it did not sound like any scramblers had entered the Fight Zone to pursue her.

"What's the Pharon?" Vesta asked.

A grim expression clouded Circe's face. She said, "Horrid creatures. The original inhabitants of this planet. Enyo keeps them under the whip and uses them as guard dogs, which is pretty funny when you see them."

Rex ordered the cage covered scrambler onto the Fight Zone. He yelled orders. The guards responded swiftly. Hasps creaked under strain and the cargo cage door slammed onto the sandy surface. A piercing shriek split the stifling air.

"Holy…" Demeter started.

"Crap!" Vesta finished.

One giant paw stepped cautiously out of the cage onto the sandy terrain. What followed was a feline shape, but also reptilian. There was a tail like a scorpion. It ended at a deadly point. Tufts of hair sprung between scales and giant whiskers rustled when the beast shrieked.

"You got to be kidding." Demeter never before bore witness to a creature so horrifying as the Pharon. She considered the Mingo Crabbes on Mongo to be the fiercest creatures in the universe. The Mingo Crabbes were no match for the indigenous species of Tartarus. Living nightmares made flesh, the Pharon made the Mingo Crabbes look like a child's pet.

The Pharon sniffed the air, detecting the fear of the nearby prisoners. She crouched, preparing to pounce, when Rex intervened with his whip. He cracked the whip across the beast's snout. Rex snapped it a second time. It flicked the beast's cheek. She hissed, eyes slitting, focusing on the bald man.

"Over there, you filthy beast." He cracked the whip again.

The Pharon sniffed the furnace-like air, detecting the delicious scent of fear pouring off Chrona. The little woman was a speck. She continued towards the rocks.

Hunched in a stalking mode, the beast leaped forward, bounding across the sand toward the fleeing figure. The spectators roared their approval. Enyo watched the wagers rise. The crowd wagered on how long Chrona had left to live, down to the second.

Terrified, Chrona felt the vibrations of the beast's heavy footfalls shake the ground beneath her before she heard them. She dared not spare a glance behind her. The fearsome creature leaped forward, its swishing tail whipping back and forth.

A video-drone swooped in for a close-up and Chrona tried batting it away. The action cost Chrona her balance. She fell with a yelp and ate a mouthful of sand.

"Chrona!" Circe moved to run to help her friend, but Demeter grabbed her shoulders and braced her. Disgusted, Circe shook herself free and turned away. She could not watch like the gawking spectators.

The dais erupted in cheers. The spectators hungered for blood and action.

Chrona struggled to regain her footing. She cried for help in Akiran, pushing herself up. She struck out at the buzzing video-drones like they were soldiers from a nest of Tracton hornets.

The woman bounded forward. If she could make it to the rocks, she could hide from the Pharon.

Mere steps away from the rocks, the very air before her became solid and electrified. The force-shield sent a bolt of electricity coursing through her body that tossed Chrona backwards through the air fifty feet.

The Pharon snatched her in midair with its mouth like she was nothing more than a treat. Rows of deadly teeth bit down on Chrona's soft body. The woman screamed in pain.

Spectators squealed with an equal mixture of horror and glee. Buzzing video-drones captured every bloody detail. The Pharon bounded back; its prey clasped between its jaws.

Enyo turned to the giant vid-screen. "Prison Planet has no fences that you can see."

The cheer thundered from the dais. Today already offered one of the better wager games in a while.

The prisoners watched helplessly as the Pharon returned. The creature approached Enyo, dropping her prize at the warden's feet. Chrona hit the ground, gasping for help. Still alive, she grabbed her tattered stomach.

"No!" Circe screamed.

"Unruliness has consequences," Rex said. His bellowing words were more for the benefit of the prisoners than the spectators. His words brought cheers from the enthusiastic crowd.

The captain of the guards whistled, and the Pharon responded, quickly snatching the wounded woman in her giant maw. With little effort, the beast bit her in half and slung her toward the center of the Fight Zone. One last scream tore from Chrona's lungs, then she fell silent, lifeless.

One feline-reptilian paw pressed onto the woman's head while the mouth began tearing the prize apart. The crowd cheered uproariously. Buzzing video-drones whizzed overhead; their unblinking cameras capturing every horrific detail.

Circe crumpled to her knees.

"Chrona, I told you not to run. I begged you not to run." She muttered to herself.

When Demeter tried to help her to her feet, Circe pushed her away.

"Get your hands off of me."

"On your feet, chippy." It was Rex.

"Leave her alone," Vesta said.

Rex raised his whip, prepared to punish both women for their acts of unruliness. Demeter stepped between the guard and the women.

Guards snapped to attention; laser pistols drawn.

"Stop. I'm getting up." Circe rose to her feet.

Rex lowered his whip. He laid a hard eyeball on the three women before speaking again.

"You chippies conserve your strength. You're going to need it."

Chapter 13:
The Kill Games

Guards ushered the beast back into its cage. Spectators placed wagers on which of the guards might fall under the Pharon's ferocity. The Pharon rocked the scrambler, bounding into the cage with the prize.

The crowd grew restless. Video-drones revealed nothing exciting. The guards finished collecting the grisly remains of the woman from the field while the crowd grumbled displeasure.

Her Eminence scowled. Enyo could not resist cursing the guards on "gut-duty." Admittedly, the Pharon had made a mess. The guards, however, could not expect the wealthy to wait all afternoon for their entertainment to resume.

"Where are the battles?" It was a cry from the restless spectators.

"We want the battles, and blood!" another shouted.

More joined in and soon they chanted, pumping their fists in the air.

"Bat-tles! Bat-tles! Bat-tles!"

The last guards left when the field was prepared. The scrambler shook and rocked with the activity of the excited Pharon inside. It pawed the remains of Chrona in its cage.

After circling the arena once, the scrambler exited the Fight Zone. Enyo stepped to the center of the screen, the robotic hand over her head. The suns gleamed off the metal and caught their waning attention. Their chanting ceased. They acted like hungry dogs, expecting a pile of meaty bones, awaiting her next word.

"My Lords, my Ladies, I promised you battle. I promised you blood."

The scrambler passed the line of prisoners. Vesta watched the covered cage rumble by. It parked beside the other scramblers. She could not stop thinking about what was inside that cage.

"It ate her," she said in a tiny voice.

Enyo pointed to the scrambler holding the Pharon. The massive vehicle stopped at the edge of the Fight Zone, the cage facing the field. This position offered the beast easier access to the Fight Zone. It was a perfect angle for the video-drones to catch all the action.

"That was only the beginning. A warm-up. A tease." Enyo enjoyed the looks of anticipation on all the expectant faces watching her from the giant screen. Soon she would have enough Mega-credits to join their ranks. Soon enough, she would be off Tartarus and living in luxury. She set her sights on Skyroid, where the most influential citizens lived. They lived in extravagant fashion, enjoying every benefit incredible wealth afforded. The denizens of Skyroid never tired of zipping off to the pleasure planets for extended holidays or keeping a staff of servants at their disposal. No longer would she have to imagine what it was like to watch the wager games from the spectator's arena. She would be among the wealthiest and most elite on the royal dais.

"Our first battle is between two prisoners you have never met, for a combat you will never forget!"

An excited murmur rumbled through the rows of spectators.

Enyo raised both hands over her head. Spinning, she turned around and pointed in all directions.

"This is the Fight Zone!"

A cheer exploded from the crowd. The giant screen quartered, each square revealing a distinct perspective of Enyo. A dry wind sent Enyo's cape billowing around her.

With a shove, Moe forced a tall, robust prisoner with a mane of frizzy blonde hair named Elara into the Fight Zone. Elara was from Xur.

It was one of the nine farming moons orbiting Akton. The planet itself was rich in natural resources and soil abundant in vital minerals to produce food, no matter how exotic. Each moon enjoyed equally enriched farming soil.

At one time, Xur had been the spouse of a simple farmer. Her day began before the twin moons made way for the morning sun and ended when the twin moons returned. Her eyes revealed a woman who had experienced a life of hardships.

Cletus snatched a slender but sinewy woman named Nyx and dragged her into the Fight Zone. Nyx called no planet, moon, or space station home. She grew up depending on her wits to survive. She was space-smart and knew how to adapt to any situation she faced.

Reluctantly, the combatants circled one another in the Fight Zone. If neither fully understood why they were in this place, they were certain of what was happening now. Only one of them was walking out of the Fight Zone with their life.

"Why are you here?" Elana called out to her opponent.

"I stole bread. You?" Nyx squinted in the brightness of the multiple suns.

"I was unruly." The bitter memory of her husband returning home after a long weekend of drinking the last of their Mega-credits flashed through her mind. The argument that followed culminated with him calling the Space Service when she became frantic. Never mind her concern for their survival. Her arrest followed, then her sentencing without benefit of counsel or judge. She wondered if he ever regretted what he did to her after sobering up. She knew it no longer mattered. Elana kicked at the hot sand.

"We are all unruly," Nyx said. She kept moving, sizing up the taller woman.

Enyo's voice boomed over the excited chatter of the spectators. "My esteemed guests. Choose your champion, and wager well."

With the simple drop of her robotic hand, the kill games began. Elana and Nyx glared at one another. They were in combat stance, hunched, arms wide, knees bent. They circled each other while the crowd cheered wildly.

"I don't want to do this," Elana said. Her eyes never left Nyx's eyes.

"I don't think we have a choice."

Both women unleashed their own war cry. They sprang, bodies smashing together, tackling the other onto the ground. The spectators responded with another boisterous cheer. The Pharon joined in with its own excited shrieking howl.

Demeter and Vesta watched, dismayed from the sidelines. Demeter assessed their situation to the best of her ability. She could not imagine any plan of action that did not end with the Pharon pouncing upon her and ripping her apart. She watched Enyo. The warden was exuberant over the wager games.

As if she could feel Demeter's eyes upon her, Enyo glanced at the warrior. The cyber-eye whirled and focused, zoomed in, and the wicked smile returned.

You'll get your chance soon enough, warrior.

Enyo turned back to the battle, then directed her attention to the wager counter. The spectators were desperate for sport and entertainment. The total number of credit-wagers soared. Spectators frantically placed bets on each combatant. Until a fighter drew first blood, the wagers would continue climbing.

"This is barbaric," Vesta said. Any fear she felt earlier was gone. There was no room for fear. The choking, stark anger roiling inside her pushed all the fear out.

"It's also why we need to find Artemis and a way out of here, fast." Demeter watched the women punch and kick each other. Blood splashed the sand. Elana snatched Nyx in a headlock, violently jerking the smaller woman around.

The spectators cheered until a gong rang out.

"Round one is complete," Enyo announced.

Nyx pushed Elana away. Both women stepped back, their chests heaving, lungs straining for breath. Each watched the other. Elana wiped the blood trickling from the corner of her mouth with the back of her hand.

Rex returned from the back of Enyo's scrambler. He carried a black box. Another cheer erupted when he unlocked it and removed the contents. He stepped into the Fight Zone long enough to thrust a laser knife into the hands of each combatant. The short blades whooshed to life. The spectators cheered.

Demeter was not paying attention to the games. She scanned the perimeter of their surroundings for at least the hundredth time. Her eyes fell upon something.

"Do you see what I see?" She nudged Vesta's arm.

Vesta watched the combatants and said, "Women who will die for no good reason?'

In a hushed tone, Demeter said, "No, look. Around the perimeter. Across from those rocks. There is a projection box. There are four projection boxes in all."

Demeter pointed in the direction opposite from where Chrona attempted to escape.

"For the force-shield." Vesta observed the rocks. The image of Chrona flying backwards from the force-shield, and the Pharon snatching her in midair, was still fresh in her memory. Near the rocks, she noticed another projector. A quick glance closer and she found the two projectors nearest their end of the Fight Zone.

"Yes, and see what's on that area beyond?" She nodded, pointing Vesta toward the direction of her gaze. There was an object obscured by heat waves between the rock formation and the force-shield projector box. Sunlight gleamed off its metallic surface.

"A ship," Vesta said excitedly. "It's a transport ship!"

The Cygnus sat beyond the force-shield projector. Demeter had not noticed before but realized it now. The transport ship brought Enyo, Zorn, other techs, and the guards that did not arrive in the prisoner transport scrambler. The warden's scrambler brought them up to the Fight Zone from the ship.

It also meant they controlled the force-shield, turning it off when the scrambler drove from the ship and entered the Fight Zone.

"Do you think you can fly it?" It was a rhetorical question, but Demeter asked anyway.

"You get me there; I can fly it," Vesta assured with great confidence. "But we're missing the cargo. Your sister, Artemis."

"You just worry about the flying. I'll worry about my sister."

Demeter's concentration snapped to the Fight Zone by the sudden booing from the spectators. She watched them on the giant vidscreen. The video-drones buzzed the air above the combatants, but there was little action to relay.

Elana and Nyx jabbed their knives. They kept moving. The laser knives whizzed in the air. An occasional slash resulted in minor damage. The wounds were superficial. The spectators craved substantial bloodshed and brutal violence. This was their recreation, after all.

"I am sorry that this is our fate," Nyx said. Sweat stung her eyes.

"The price for bread is too high here," Elana responded.

Rex entered the Fight Zone. He shoved Elana toward Nyx. When Nyx realized the other woman was about to fall onto her laser knife blade, she reflexively flicked it out of the way. A fresh round of boos and jeers erupted from the crowd.

"Put your guts in it, chippies," Rex taunted and laughed. Harsh sunlight reflected off his bare scalp.

With a ferocious war cry, Elana jabbed left with all her might. She aimed the blade toward Rex's bloated, ugly, bald head. She wanted to drive the blade's laser point into his brain, but the big captain was faster than she expected. He dodged the blade. It missed his head before finding Nyx's throat.

The spectators were on their feet, half cheering and applauding, while others looked miserable, angrily crumpling their losing wager tickets. Enyo smiled, the cyber-eye scanning the satisfied crowd on the vid-screen.

The Pharon shrieked in its cargo cage. All the sudden excitement made it agitated. It smelled fresh blood.

Surprise colored Nyx's face. She went silent in an open-mouth gasp. She took a step forward, her eyes locking on Elana's.

The gong rang out, announcing the end of the bout, but it was not the end. Nyx stood frozen until at last her legs became rubbery. Her eyes were wide with shock, her mouth fixed in a silent scream. Blood sizzled around the laser knife's blade. The smallest trickle of blood ran between her fingers. She could only stare blankly at Elana and wait for the Great Reaper to take her to the next realm.

Rex raised Elana's hand in victory. All the simple farmer's wife from Xur could do was mouth the words "I'm sorry." Tears filled her eyes. She watched Nyx fall onto the burning sand.

Laughing, Rex retrieved the laser knife from Nyx's throat.

When the spectators could wait no longer, the cargo cage door fell open, and the Pharon leaped out. Hairs bristling between her scales, the creature took one cautious step forward. The beast considered Rex and Elana, sniffed the air, then Enyo and the crowd that had fallen silent on the screen behind her. It sniffed again. The beast leaped; found Nyx's body and snatched the woman up. It bounded back into the cargo cage.

A jubilant cheer of approval erupted from the dais.

Rex wrapped Elana in one giant arm and dragged her out of the Fight Zone. She could barely walk and could not keep up with the captain. She tripped over her feet while the captain dragged her along.

"How much can that thing eat?" Vesta asked.

"It's not for her," Circe said. "She's taking it to feed to her younglings."

Circe laughed when she saw Vesta shudder.

Enyo stepped into the center of the Fight Zone, peering up at the spectators. Sunlight reflected off the cyber-eye. She scanned every disgusting, expectant expression of glee and satisfaction.

"Did that please you, my honored guests?" A roar of approval thundered throughout the wasteland.

"I trust you wagered well. And you will want to be even more generous with your purse for the next match."

Enyo turned from the crowd, arms raised and announced, "Today we have a truly magnificent fighter, a gladiator who is a hard criminal and a Fight Zone favorite."

A murmur of anticipation broke out among the spectators.

She approached the prisoners, moving at a leisurely pace, dragging out the moment for the benefit of delicious suspense. Her guests hung on her every word with frenzied anticipation.

The cyber-eye scanned across faces until it finally locked on the face for which it searched. She turned to her audience and announced, "Circe!"

Her robotic hand pointed out Circe among the fighters. The woman took a step forward. She bowed her head to the cheers.

Rex dragged Elana toward the other prisoners and dropped her. The woman teetered on unconsciousness. When she asked for water, he laughed, turning his attention to Enyo.

"And she will battle her archenemy, the unruly and notorious bounty hunter Vesta!"

The cyber-eye scrutinized Demeter's face, breaking it down into squares and examining each one. The warrior shot Enyo a challenging look. She wanted to rip the smile from the warden's face. The cyber-eye buzzed, examining the prisoner beside her.

The robotic hand grabbed Vesta out of the line of prisoners.

"Oh, no," Demeter said. Her voice was a whisper.

Cletus and Moe approached and took her from the warden. They dragged Vesta into the Fight Zone. The pilot struggled the entire way.

Spectators began placing their bets.

"This is an insult," Circe cried. "I want Demeter, not her wimpy pilot!"

The guards readied their laser pistols and waited to dole out punishment. Insubordination always resulted in punishment. Enyo motioned for them to stand down.

"Dispatch this one and you can have the other one." Enyo spoke directly to Circe. It was a command.

Before another word passed between them, the gong rang. It was time for battle.

The two combatants circled each other.

"All right, let's make this fast," Circe said. In the blazing multiple suns, her tattoo and scar covered body came alive in the shimmering heat waves. The heat waves made the tattoos appear to move across her flesh, slipping over and under the scars, like a video-play on a vid-screen cassette tape.

"Agreed. The Pharons need to be fed," Vesta said. She did not sound as brave as she hoped.

Vesta controlled her breathing, steadied her heart rate.

All of Demeter's training suddenly exploded into the forefront of her brain. She kept her eyes fastened on Circe to predict the woman's next move. Demeter always said that if you read your opponent's eyes, you could predict their next move.

Vesta prepared herself for Circe's attack. The woman sprang. Vesta pivoted on her left foot, preventing Circe from snatching her in a headlock. The women hopped from one foot to the other, then made their move. They clashed, grabbing each other, and pummeling with tight fists. Vesta gave it as hard as she took it, and a lucky uppercut landed on Circe's jaw. Surprised, Circe wavered on her feet, which gave Vesta the opportunity to land an expert jab to her nose.

Pain erupted throughout Circe's skull. She retaliated with a raging storm of body blows and leg sweeps. When Circe prepared to drop a heavy leg across Vesta's neck, the pilot spun and took the woman's legs out from under her. She fell hard and Vesta landed a knee on her head, smashing Circe's face into the blistering sand.

The spectators cheered. Enyo watched the bout with great interest. The video-drones showed how quickly the pilot gained the upper hand. Circe never fell to an opponent like that before.

Circe twisted, threw a handful of sand into Vesta's face, and wriggled out from under the pilot. Vesta lost her balance and her advantage.

Demeter wanted to jump in and help her partner, but three of the guards had their laser pistols aimed at her.

"Laser knife fight!" A voice cried out. Soon, all the spectators joined the chanting, "Laser knife fight! Laser knife fight!"

"Finally. Now I can finish you," Circe said.

Was the gong ever going to ring? Vesta thought. She wiped hot sand out of her teary eyes with the palms of her hands.

Circe produced her shiv out of thin air and swiped at Vesta.

Where did she get that?

Vesta expertly jumped out of the path of the deadly sliver of metal. She dodged the blade by a hair. She scanned the zone frantically. Rex stood with his muscled arms crossed. There was no knife, laser or otherwise, forthcoming.

Circe leaped, the shiv swishing mere inches from Vesta's face. Vesta acted quickly, grabbing Circe's wrist with both hands and jerking it behind the woman's back. The shiv fell uselessly to the sand. She kicked the woman's legs out from under her. Circe landed face first into the hot sand for a second time. Vesta had the advantage again and wrenched her opponent's arm back until pain exploded in Circe's shoulder.

"You fight dirty," Vesta said. The sand granules still stinging her eyes. Her anger was in full control now.

"I fight to live," Circe said. She winced; more pain erupting in her shoulder when Vesta did not care for her response.

Enyo laughed. It was not time for a new champion.

The gong sounded.

The screen showed the spectators. They waved their wager tickets in the air. They called for blood, demanding that Vesta finish the bout despite the gong having sounded.

"Finish her!"

More voices joined the ruckus.

Vesta looked down at Circe. She no longer struggled. The shiv glinted in the sand, sparkling in the sunlight. It was close enough to grab and finish the job.

It's right there, Vesta thought.

"Don't," Demeter said. Dread seized her heart.

The expression that blazed across the pilot's face was ferocious. It would be easy to finish it, but at what cost? Was this what she wanted to be, a killer of women?

"Finish her," Enyo's voice boomed. Bound by duty, the warden had to grant the wishes of her spectators, even at the cost of her champion. It was not what she wanted, but it was what they wanted, and the spectators were always right.

When the blood craving of the crowd was at its most frenzied, Vesta looked up and noticed the video-drones buzzing overhead. She saw her own image, four images, in fact, from different angles, on the giant vid-screen. The images made her stomach turn.

I fight to live, is what her opponent had said to her. Those words haunted Vesta.

A new outcome for the battle revealed itself to her. She climbed off of Circe.

"Then live," she said.

Confusion filled Circe by the unexpected outcome. Vesta offered a hand and helped her up. She eyed the shiv for only a moment and then looked at Enyo.

"I don't fight dirty," Vesta said. Her voice grew stronger with each word.

The crowd expressed their disappointment. It was clear the names they were calling Vesta, as well as Circe and even Enyo, were not endearments.

The warden was not happy. She motioned for Rex to take control of the situation.

The captain rushed into the Fight Zone, whip in hand. Moe and

Cletus pulled their laser pistols free, ready to blast Vesta into a mess of charred bones. The spectators always enjoyed that.

Rex jerked Circe out of the way when Demeter appeared, determined to help her partner. She smashed a fist into Rex's ugly face. The blow caught him completely off guard and sent him crashing onto his butt. He dropped the whip and Demeter snatched it from the sand.

The crowd roared at the turn of events. Before Enyo responded to the attack, the wager counter jumped. New wagers drove the counter numbers higher. The spectators bet on the prisoners against her guards.

Circe watched in amazement. Demeter and Vesta fought side by side, backs to one another, trusting the other to cover them. Demeter snapped the whip and popped one guard before he could free his sidearm. He went down screaming, clutching his bloodied wrist. The crowd rose out of their seats cheering.

Rather than watch, Circe snatched the shiv and joined the bounty hunters in combat. A guard rushed her. She hunched her body down and sprang up, tossing him backwards. She scrambled on top of him and freed his laser pistol.

Vesta delivered a roundhouse kick into another guard's head, cracking his helmet in half. He dropped to the sand with a vicious ringing in his ears.

More guards entered the fray. The women fought until the guards overpowered them. They were on the women, punching and kicking. It took everything all of the guards had to restrain only three women.

The crowd booed when the battle ended, and not in the favor of the warrior women.

Rex grabbed a laser pistol from one of his guards and put it to Demeter's head.

"Stop!" Enyo commanded. Her robotic hand rose, halting him. All eyes were on Rex. Spectators wagered on what the captain would do next.

"Take these unruly prisoners to the decontamination chamber!"

Chapter 14:
Warriors in Chains

Silent and chained, the three women stood against the decontamination chamber wall. Sweat poured in rivulets down their dirty faces. Each was shackled around their right wrist. Their arms were pulled high enough they were on the balls of their feet. Breathing was difficult. The humidity was thick; it seemed to press down upon them, smothering them.

Unlike the previous day, only a few light bars radiated illumination. Dark, the chamber was a dungeon. Unimaginable tortures transpired in this place. Demeter no longer wondered what the spatters of filth were.

"I'm beginning to hate this spa," Vesta said. Her tone was normal, tinged with sarcasm. Demeter knew that any fear Vesta felt earlier was gone.

"Just stick to the plan," Demeter said.

"Plan? What plan?" Circe was interested in their discussion. "There is no escape from Prison Planet."

"For you maybe, bitchy-big-shot. You seem to like it here," Vesta said.

"I don't get it. Why did you spare my life?" Circe craned her neck to look past Demeter and see Vesta.

The Wolfhound's pilot shrugged. Her chain rattled with the effort.

"Vesta does the wrong things for the right reasons," Demeter said. She heard the pilot stifle a laugh.

"You two are pathetic." Circe shook her head. "Like that other chippy they brought in."

"What other chippy?" Demeter asked.

Circe ignored her while she twisted her body to retrieve the shiv from its hiding place under her gown. She kept it under her arm. The guards were too dumb to check there whenever they patted her down.

Raising her free hand over her head, she picked the shackle lock with the blade's point. She strained to reach it. She noticed both women staring at her, waiting for her to continue.

"Astra, Adriadna, something like that," she said.

"Artemis?" Demeter asked.

Circe stopped picking at the lock. A thoughtful expression filled her face. She nodded.

"Yeah, sounds right. Pretty. Rex took a liking to her. They've been keeping her out of gen pop, in another cellblock."

Circe noted the look between the women.

"She means something to you?" Circe asked. When the warrior did not respond, she resumed picking the lock.

"She's my sister," Demeter said, her voice flat.

A metallic pop sounded, followed by the clanking of the heavy shackle hitting the chamber wall. Circe rubbed her freed wrist.

"I said I owed you a debt of your own blood. Well, now, I owe this one a debt of my life." She nodded toward Vesta.

"What does that mean?" Demeter asked. She was more than a little suspicious of Circe's intentions.

"It means I owe her a debt of loyalty, and I won't kill you in your sleep."

"You'll help me find my sister?" Demeter asked.

"I will help *her* find your sister and get off this hell of a planet." Circe cocked a brow.

"It won't be easy," Demeter said.

"That's the only thing we can count on."

The chamber door creaked open. Enyo swaggered in. She held Rex's whip in the hand made of flesh and bone. It dragged along the cold concrete floor behind her. She peered at the three women. The cyber-eye revealed Circe was free of her shackle and hid something behind her back. Probably the shiv. It was of no concern to Enyo.

"You three made a real mess of my wager games."

They averted their eyes away from the warden. The mechanical eye whirled like a security camera, clicking electronically, scanning each of them.

"Lucky for you, Her Eminence may forgive. If we provide a great kill, next match."

Enyo used the whip handle to raise Vesta's chin so she could look the younger woman in the eyes. The cyber-eye studied the pilot's features, the focus and zoom rings adjusting with a gentle buzz.

"What I don't understand is why you didn't finish her today."

Vesta looked away.

Enyo pulled the whip away. She continued.

"I looked you up. At least I tried to look you up. You two aren't in the criminal database."

Enyo squeezed the whip handle. Demeter heard the leather squeak under the stress. It seemed the cyclopean warden was fondling the whip.

"It's all very mysterious. You are ghosts." She paused a moment. "Only, I don't believe in ghosts."

With a speed no one expected, Enyo snapped the whip at Vesta. It cracked and sent a stinging pain flaring up her right arm. Vesta cried out.

"Tell me why you're here!"

"Leave her alone," Demeter said.

The tip of the whip snapped dangerously close to Demeter's face. It could easily take her eye out. She jerked away from it.

"Then you tell me who you are and why you're here." Enyo snapped the whip again.

Calm your mind. Think rationally.

Demeter pushed the immediate anger down, as it would do her no good in their current situation. She stared at Enyo and said, "We're unruly prisoners on your prison planet."

Enyo snapped the whip more viciously. Its tip found flesh and delivered stinging bolts of pain. Fury raged within her. She snapped the whip repeatedly until she was out of breath.

"Spies! I think you are spies for the law!"

"You mean the law that arrested us and sent us here?" Circe stepped forward. The shiv glinted in the dull light.

Enyo turned her attention to her champion.

"You know a lot about this."

The cyber-eye whirled, clicked, and focused.

Enyo cracked the whip with a surgeon's precision. The tip lashed out and sent a hot sting across Circe's left cheek. Before the tattooed woman reacted, the tip lashed across her right cheek. Beads of blood dribbled from the slashes in her flesh.

Like a serpent acting on its own accord, the whip snapped overhead and struck again. It wrapped itself around Circe's throat and jerked the champion toward her. The shiv dropped.

Circe felt the warden's hot breath on her stinging cheeks.

"Why were you spared?" Enyo demanded.

When no answer came, Enyo twisted the whip tighter. Agonizing pain exploded throughout Circe's body.

"Answer me!"

Circe accepted the punishment. She could not breathe, and she tasted blood, but she stared defiantly into the warden's robotic eye. Her reflection mouthed a silent curse before she had enough strength to speak.

"She who fights and runs may turn and fight another day." It was a hoarse choke, and she knew she used the last breath she would get before she fell unconscious to the floor.

"But she who is in battle slain, will never rise to fight again," Vesta said.

"Tacitus. We are the ghosts of Tacitus," Demeter said.

Enyo held Circe in the death choke a stretch longer, then released her. The champion fell to the chamber floor, chocking.

Enyo pointed a robotic finger at the prisoners.

"Ghosts or spies, you are criminals now. And you may be too clever to leave a record, but I will sniff you out."

With the flick of her wrist, the tip of the whip jumped into her hand. She expertly coiled the whip by snapping her wrist three times.

Her grip tightened, forcing the leather to stress under the compression and squeak. Sighing, Enyo turned and left the chamber without further comment. The door slammed behind her.

When Circe caught her breath, she retrieved the shiv and used it to free Vesta and Demeter.

"Thanks," Vesta said, rubbing her wrist.

"The enemy of my enemy is my friend. And that bitch Enyo is my enemy." Circe nodded.

Chapter 15:
A Wager

Where am I?

Artemis did not know where she was. Since her banishment to the prison planet, she spent her incarceration in a giant, windowless chamber with a dozen other women. Rows of hanging illumination bars radiated murky light. Each of the women spent their time lounging on dirty mattresses, amid mounds of dirty pillows. They had been pretty at once. This rancid place spoiled their beauty.

Beauty has no place here, she thought.

Girls came and went. Guards appeared, called out names, then disappeared. Half the girls returned. The fate of the others remained a mystery. They suspected the women who did not return stood at the side of the Great Reaper.

Artemis gave up on escaping. There was no escape. The ceiling reached too high to climb. The single door remained bolted. She lost all sense of time in the eternal gloom.

She sat on the edge of her mattress, absently running a brush through her hair. Her hair, once full and robust, was flat and knotty. She pulled the brush through the tangled mess. There was nothing else to do.

Leda, a buxom brunette, rushed to her side. She was the only one who talked to her.

"Have you heard? A prisoner refused to finish her opponent in the kill games today," she said in an excited flurry of words.

Artemis perked up.

"Really? Do you know her name?"

"No, but she was a new unruly that just arrived."

"Too much to ask," Artemis muttered to herself.

"What?" Leda asked.

Artemis hesitated a moment. She knew it was wrong to wish for Demeter's help. This time it was bad.

"That my sister has come for me," she said. Her voice became lost in the vast chamber.

Leda offered a sad smile. She brushed a wisp of hair behind Artemis's ear, then cupped the side of her face in a motherly gesture.

"Don't get your hopes up," Leda said. "Even if it is your sister, she'll never get you off this planet."

"Want to wager?" Artemis asked. Her eyes were aglow with hope.

"What do I win?" Leda watched her.

Artemis noticed the hairbrush in her hand and held it up.

"My hairbrush." The golden brush sparkled like a precious treasure in the gloom.

"And what do you win?" Leda asked.

"My freedom."

The chamber door opened. Neander entered. His laser pistol drawn and ready.

"On your feet, prisoner." He barked repeatedly until Artemis realized he was yelling at her. He jabbed the laser pistol in her direction.

"What do you want?" Leda asked. She made no move toward Artemis or the guard. The penalty for defending a fellow inmate was severe. She was not, however, afraid to question Neander.

"None of your concern," Neander said.

"She needs her rest. Tomorrow is Pair Day," the brunette said.

"Quiet, chippy." His dead eyes focused on the prisoner Artemis. Retrieving the prisoner as instructed overrode all other thoughts in his mind. Nothing could stop him.

Artemis rose from the mattress.

She felt exposed in the tattered gown. She hugged her arms to cover herself. For only a second, she wondered if she could wrestle the weapon away from him.

"Move," Neander said.

Worry colored Leda's face. She almost spoke.

"It's all right, Leda. I will comply," Artemis said.

"Good," Neander said. "Captain wants to see you in his quarters."

Leda looked dismayed but said nothing.

Artemis observed the expression shadowing Leda's face. Dread gnawed at her. She knew the number of girls taken to the captain that never returned.

"Have I done anything wrong?" Artemis asked. She wondered if he even saw her standing before her with such empty eyes. He looked restless.

"I have my orders. Now move it!"

Artemis handed the hairbrush to Leda.

"Hold on to this and remember our wager."

Leda took the brush and nodded. She whispered, "Our wager."

Neander grabbed Artemis by the arm and dragged her out of the chamber cell.

The captain waited.

Chapter 16:
Beauty and the Brute

Artemis marched through the dark corridors, trying to keep up with Neander's pace. Her bare feet found every rock and sharp piece of debris along the way. She winced repeatedly. The guard refused to slow down. They crossed the grounds, coming into an open space of buildings. Ramshackle quarters lined one side.

A vast dome covered the area, blocking out the multiple suns. Illumination bars on tall poles lit the area. The place was deserted.

Little more than a row of dilapidated shacks, each unit housed a dozen guards. She imagined the squalor inside the shacks. Rex, however, enjoyed living quarters much grander than the rest of the quarters combined. Majestic by comparison, his housing sat at the end of the line of shacks.

It reminded her of the ancient western towns depicted on some of the vid-screen cassette tape dramas she watched for entertainment.

Neander shoved Artemis forward after opening the grand entrance. She stumbled inside. Her feet slapped on cold stone tiles. She heard the door squeak shut behind her. Astonishment filled her upon entering the new environment.

The interior reminded her of one of Lord Colwyn's tented oases on the edge of the Black Forest of Glaive. It was luxurious in ways she never believed possible in such a hellish world. It smelled of flowers that would never survive the planet's desert terrain.

Grand orbs of illumination swayed on long, glittery chains. Curtains and swags and beaded ropes hung decoratively about. The furniture was grand, crafted for a man of girth. The craftsmanship was impeccable. A pot of simmering oil filled the air with the flowery scent.

This is weird.

This is the lair of a predator.

Rex greeted her from the floor. He sat among a pile of pillows; clean, fluffy plush pillows. He smiled. Before him was a table laid out with delicious cuisine.

"There you are!" He spoke with surprise to see her. It was the first time she had seen him without the helmet and mask. His head was bald and clean. He had full eyebrows and was almost handsome in a brutish way. Something about his smile made her queasy.

How coy he is, she thought. Removed from his armor, he wore a flowing red and purple robe, cinched at his great stomach with a leather rope belt and leather slippers on his feet.

Even relaxing, Rex appeared fearsome. He seemed out of place among the finery of the extravagant furnishings.

Artemis hesitated, stalling a moment longer where she stood, trying to make sense of her current situation.

"Please, sit down," he said, gesturing for her to join him. Next to him was an arrangement of pillows awaiting her.

She took a seat on an fluffy pillow of lavender and gold. It felt wonderful compared to the lumpy, dirty mattress she slept on in the chamber.

"As you can see, I appreciate fine things." He sipped from a golden bejeweled goblet and smacked his lips. His smile never faltered.

I bet it's the cheapest swill he could find; she thought.

Barrels of that rotgut whiskey Klytus sold throughout the galaxy to space pirates and scavengers for nothing. They named the concoction after the miner who boiled up the first batch. He stayed behind after the mines on Io dried up. Klytus was cheap to make and cheap to buy.

She was right. She watched Rex pour the blue-hued alcohol into another goblet. When the liquor filled the goblet halfway, he handed it to her.

"What is your name?" he asked. His voice was softer than usual. She knew it was a ruse.

"Artemis," she answered. She looked at the blue liquid in the goblet. Did she dare drink it? A sip or two of the cheap liquor would soften her defenses. She did not want to be any more vulnerable in the company of this man than she had to be.

"Well, Artemis, I am Rex, captain of the guards." He bowed his head.

"Yes, sir."

The big man leaned closer to her.

"No need to be so formal. Call me Rex."

"All right. Rex." She had a bad feeling.

"Good," he leaned back. "Now let me ask you, how has your stay been so far? Treated well? Food to your liking?"

This creep had to be kidding. Artemis looked away from him. She felt smothered under his unblinking gaze.

"Yes, sir."

Rex twisted his substantial body and caught her eye. He reached for her.

She felt his rough, callused fingertips on her chin, drawing her gaze to meet his.

"No need for lies. I know Prison Planet is a hellhole. And mostly hellions come here to rot."

Rex scooted closer to her, pushing pillows out of his way, and sliding his entire body next to hers. He was close enough for Artemis to feel his body heat on her, followed by the musky scent of cologne. It made him smell sour. His fetid breath coated her, and she stomped down the urge to retch.

Please don't kiss me with that puke breath.

An inch from her face, he stopped.

"But every once in a while, a lovely creature arrives. A rare butterfly who lands to grace us with her beauty."

Rex poured more of the blue liquid into her goblet. She had yet to take the first sip.

"Prison Planet doesn't have to be horrible. It can be pleasant and wonderful. I can make it pleasant and wonderful for you, Artemis."

Artemis stared intently at the liquid in the goblet. Then his rough hands stroked her hair as gently as they performed any task of punishment.

"Well, sir," Artemis began, her voice low and quavering. She raised her head to look directly at him. "I don't wish to be unruly, but I play for the other team."

Rex considered this. He looked more amused than alarmed.

"I can live with that." His grin nauseated her.

"I can't," she said.

A cloud of agitation crossed his face. She saw instant anger in his eyes.

"You're making a big mistake." His voice lost whatever gentle tone it had.

"My big mistake was getting sent to this place," she said.

Rex snarled. He stood quickly. His face turned a bright crimson and Artemis saw veins bulging across his forehead.

"Guard!" he shouted.

Neander rushed in without hesitation, weapon drawn.

"Sir," the guard responded. His lifeless eyes showed nothing but obedience.

"Take this chippy back to her cell."

Neander moved quickly, jerking Artemis to her feet. She cried out, a bolt of pain exploding in her shoulder.

"Spend more time on Prison Planet and experience all its horrors," the captain said. Venom dripped from each word. He bellowed like he wanted every prisoner in the compound to hear his words. "Soon you'll be begging me to take my offer!"

With a wave, he dismissed them. Neander pulled her along. She lost her footing stepping over the mounds of pillows, but the guard held her upright.

"You'll come around soon enough. For now, sleep with the dung rats, and get ready to fight for your life on Pair Day."

Chapter 17:
The Protective Mother

The Pharon stirred in her den. She nosed another piece of meat toward her younglings. They snapped at the remains of Nyx and Chrona, tearing the flesh free from the bones. They ate, their little jaws grinding the meat.

When they finished, they nuzzled close to their mother. She groomed them with her serpentine tongue. The beast licked over scales and tufts of hair and the young Pharons purred. The mother sat with her scorpion-like tail wrapped around their small bodies, the deadly tip tucked beneath her.

The younglings fell asleep in her embrace. An instinct in its feline-reptilian brain knew they needed to grow bigger and stronger. It was their mother's hope that they grew to defy the puny little creatures with the cages and the whips and the burning rays of light. She vowed the little creatures would never abuse her younglings like they abused her.

The Pharon hated the little creatures. She remembered when there were no tiny creatures and only her own species ruled the planet.

If it were not that the tiny creatures kept them fed on their own delicious meat, she would have destroyed them and reclaimed the planet. The once proud creatures perished at the hands of the tiny creatures. The Pharons became extinct. But for now, she had her young to attend. If anything happened to her, they would be helpless to care for themselves.

The Pharon rose, careful not to awaken her young. She moved out of the cool darkness of their den into the heat of the multiple suns. The heat felt good on her scales. Purring like the younglings, she saw the one called Tycho near the cage door. Her purring ceased. She shrieked into the stifling air.

Tycho drew his laser pistol.

"Shut up, you filthy beast!"

So puny, the Pharon thought. *So tiny and fragile. I could snatch and swallow the little creature easily; does he not know that?*

The Pharon stared at the guard. He was always there, always yelling at her, spitting, and antagonizing her. The little creature advanced, ready to hurt her with the beams of stinging light.

Her hair bristled and her haunches rose. Her tail whipped back and forth. She contemplated ending the life of this pathetic little creature. It would be so easy, and then she would awaken the younglings and feed his tasty little body to them.

The younglings.

She had to protect her younglings. They could not care for themselves yet. She could not risk abandoning them just for the joy of crushing one puny creature. The others would surely come and possibly destroy them all. She could not allow that to happen.

Another ear-piercing shriek filled the air and then the Pharon backed away, returning to the den.

Chapter 18:
A Plan of Action

The Pharon's shriek echoed throughout the dark cellblock.

"Do they do that every night?" Vesta asked.

"As long as I've been here," Circe said.

The shrieking ceased.

Circe's crew huddled around her, Vesta, and Demeter. Aero, a beautiful dark-skinned woman with a muscular physique and a golden mane of hair, sat on the bunk next to Circe.

"What's the deal, Circe? You make friends with bounty hunters now?" Aero did not trust Demeter or Vesta. She considered them no better than a member of the Space Service.

"Allies, not friends," Circe corrected. "And stay close, because there are security cameras watching."

"We have a plan to break out, but we need your help," Demeter said in a hushed tone.

Aero snorted and smirked.

"No one breaks out," the dark-skinned woman said. She crossed her arms across her chest, regarding Demeter and her partner with disgust.

Circe retrieved the shiv from its hiding place and cut her palm. She cut Demeter's palm in the same manner before the warrior protested.

She clasped their hands together.

"We are blood now. If Demeter says we break out, we break out." She challenged the surrounding women with a stern look. They regarded her for a silent moment. Aero nodded and held her tongue.

"Or would you rather stay here?" Circe asked.

The women considered this, glancing from one to the other. They turned back to their leader, mouths shut.

Circe said, "I didn't think so."

"So, what's this plan of yours?" Aero asked. Her eyes burned into Demeter.

"We need weapons, and we need to get to the other cellblock."

"I have my knife," Circe offered. "The guards have weapons."

"We don't need to get to the other cellblock," Elana said.

"What do you mean?" Demeter watched the tall, blonde-haired woman.

"They'll be bringing prisoners from the other cellblock to the Fight Zone for the next game. They do it every other fight. It's called Pair Day. Fresh blood."

Demeter's flesh crawled at the thought of Artemis being forced into the Fight Zone. She was pretty sure her baby sister never managed a weapon deadlier than a paintbrush in her life.

"All right. Then we're ready for Vesta to employ her special skills." She turned to her partner.

"Right now?" Vesta was not ready. "I'm tired from the kill games and, frankly, I'm starving."

Circe snapped her fingers. At once, Aero offered Vesta a pathetic chunk of bread. They smuggled it from dinner and saved it for just such an occasion.

"It's all we have," Aero said.

Vesta took the bread and broke it in half. She returned the other half to Aero.

"This is more than enough," she said. Without hesitation, she put the bread in her mouth and chewed. It was dry as the surface of Tartarus. It took extreme effort to chew it into a palpable lump. The bread absorbed all the moisture in her mouth.

"Are you ready yet?" Demeter asked impatiently.

Vesta held a finger up.

"Just a minute." She chewed the gritty lump of bread.

With effort, she swallowed. It felt scratchy going down.

"Ready," the pilot said, nodded.

Vesta suddenly crumpled to the floor. Eyes wide, she clutched her throat, rolling on the floor, choking. Her face turned blue; eyes bulged. She gasped. Her throat and airways swelled, leaving her lungs straining from lack of oxygen.

"The bread wasn't that bad," Aero said. Panic seized her and the rest of Circe's crew.

"Guard! Guard!" Demeter continued shouting until she heard them approach. "We need help now!"

Moe and Cletus appeared. They approached the disturbance, hands clutching the handles of their sidearms.

"What's the commotion?" Moe demanded in a monotone voice.

"There's something wrong with her," Demeter said. She pointed to Vesta on the floor, who was now motionless. A line of thick saliva ran out of her mouth, down her cheek, and onto the cellblock floor.

Both guards entered the cellblock. Cletus pulled his laser pistol and kept it trained on Demeter. Moe crouched on one knee, inspecting the prisoner. He turned her head one way and then the other. Her eyes rolled back into her head.

"She the one who fought today?" he asked.

"Yes," Demeter said, her words a rush. "She may have internal injuries. Please help."

Moe contemplated whether it was worth turning on the Biotron Medi-droid to scan her guts. To Cletus he said, "What do you think?"

"Not our problem," he answered, same monotone voice. "Leave her there. If she's dead by morning, we'll give her to the Pharons." His gaze never left Demeter and the other women.

"Unruliness has consequences," Moe said. It was his final assessment of the situation. He stood, done dealing with the situation.

"Let's go," Cletus said. His dull eyes trained on the women.

Exiting, they were careful none of the women escaped. The cell door slammed shut behind them. The clang of metal-on-metal rang throughout the cellblock. Cletus stabbed the key into the lock and secured it for the night.

"Go to sleep," he commanded. They turned and left.

It did not surprise Circe or her crew that the guards left Vesta to die. Such disregard for life was part of their world.

Vesta popped up with a grin, startling everyone except Demeter. Her face returned to its natural color.

"Feeling better?" Demeter asked. She knew it was all an act. She helped Vesta into a sitting position.

Vesta patted her back. Concealed from the prying eyes of the security cameras behind the women, she revealed the outline of Moe's laser pistol under her gown.

"I am indeed. You could say I am well armed to face tomorrow's battles."

The deception impressed Circe. "That was some fine fakery, bounty hunter."

"We're not out of the woods yet," Vesta reminded them.

"No, but when we get my sister, we'll not only get out, but we'll set fire to the woods if we have to," Demeter said.

The women huddled closer and discussed the plan for the following day's wager games.

Chapter 19:
Pair Day

After a rugged journey across brutal terrain, the prisoners stumbled off the scrambler. Guards directed them to line up along the edge of the Fight Zone. Today would be a special Pair Day event.

The humongous vid-screen rose, revealing the privileged spectators for the day's entertainment. A video-drone scanned the crowd and then stopped, revealing the empty chair of Her Eminence.

"Enyo can't be happy that Her Eminence is a no-show," Cerci said.

Demeter nodded toward the warden's distant transport ship. Today it was the Palomino.

"Quiet. Focus. That's our target," she said.

Enyo appeared in the center of the Fight Zone like a demented ringmaster presiding over her circus of terror. Her green cape billowed around her.

"Lords and Ladies. My esteemed guests. I am honored to have you here on Pair Day."

Video-drones zoomed overhead. They captured every angle of the warden. A wild rumble rose from the crowd. They cheered with demented glee.

Demeter watched for another scrambler transporting the

prisoners from the other cellblock to appear. The only other vehicle was the caged cargo scrambler containing the Pharon. The beast was unusually quiet.

"On Pair Day," Enyo continued, "we match the most savage fighters from each cellblock, and blow by blow, pare them down."

A thunder of uproarious applause erupted across the vid-screen. Enyo's cyber-eye scanned the crowd of eager faces. She could practically smell their wealth. They screamed, waved their hands, and cheered. Today, they would see blood.

"Where is Artemis?" Demeter said. She was becoming agitated. Her plan was already falling apart. Where was the other scrambler?

"Cool your jets, bounty hunter. She will be here," Circe said.

Demeter fidgeted from one foot to the other. She grew restless.

"But first," Enyo's voice boomed. "We have a new entertainment for you."

"This is new," Circe said, curious.

"Behold. The jester prisoners!"

Rex stepped into the center of the Fight Zone, dragging two smaller prisoners like dogs on chains. They were dregs from the solitary confinement block. They were filthy and animal-like. Multiple suns burned eyes that had long grown accustomed to darkness.

A cheer burst from the spectators.

The captain was without his helmet and face mask. He looked exhausted. His bare head glistened with sweat in the suns. His smile was cruel, twisting in such a way it showed no mirth, only menace.

He removed the collars, revealing the glittery colorful clown frill underneath. Garish make-up colored their faces. Someone haphazardly smeared red and blue makeup on their cheeks, nose and around their dark eyes. They looked like clowns from an underworld carnival.

The prisoners appeared absolutely terrified. This brought more joy to the spectators. Both had been crying, and they jumped when Rex snapped his whip. The big captain roared with laughter.

Enyo encouraged the spectators to join in the fun. Was there anything more entertaining?

The warden whipped them into a frenzy. The wealthy, the elite, and the privileged guffawed at the spectacle.

From a pouch attached around his waist, Rex retrieved a meaty bone. He held it over his head.

A new cheer grew from the spectators. They began wagering on the outcome of what would happen next.

"Is that a…" Vesta's voice stopped. She could not bear to continue her thought. Rex paraded the bone around the Fight Zone for all to see.

The video-drones locked on the chunk of meat and bone, projecting every detail across the big screen.

Flesh clinging to the bone revealed a tattoo of a four-armed spiral. Chrona got the tattoo to prove her loyalty to Circe. All the women in Circe's gang had them.

With a flick, Rex tossed the bone into the Fight Zone. It landed between the jester prisoners. All the humiliations of their incarceration and the tortures of the last six hours vanished. Hunger, similar to madness, drove them like an engine and they pounced to snatch the morsel.

A cheer rose from the crowd, followed by more laughter. The prisoners wrestled in the hot sand for the bone. They pulled and punched, ripped it from each other just for a taste of the red meat.

"Look at those gluttons," a woman on the dais called out. More jeers and comments followed.

The video-drones recorded every antic for the crowd's delight. When Enyo thought they had enough, she gestured for Rex to collect the prisoners and remove them from the Fight Zone.

Enyo approached the chosen fighters for the Pair Day games while her captain collected the jesters. He pushed them apart, but savage instinct overrode all else and they continued wrestling for the bone.

Jeers and laughter continued. Rex struggled momentarily to corral both women. The crack of his whip stopped them. They ceased; the bone forgotten. The memory of the recent floggings at the hands of the sadistic captain froze them where they stood.

Blood and half chewed chunks of raw meat smeared their painted faces.

Enyo's cyber-eye scanned the prisoners waiting to enter the

Fight Zone and stopped at Demeter. The warrior glared at her. She wanted to rip Enyo's head off and drop kick it into the suns.

Good, Enyo thought. *Use that rage in the games today, warrior.*

Vesta flinched at the captain's cruelty toward the prisoners in the Fight Zone. Rex slapped them across their heads, reconnecting the collars. She watched helplessly as he jerked them forward, dragging them into motion. When he detected the slightest resistance, he struck them across their bare legs with his whip.

"Those poor prisoners. They don't deserve that," Vesta said.

"Don't mix in, Vesta," Demeter said.

Rex raised the whip to strike the jester prisoners again.

When she could no longer stand by and watch, Vesta bolted into the Fight Zone.

"Leave them alone!" she shouted.

The crowd fell silent. They placed wagers on the outcome of the little red-headed prisoner's outburst.

Taken by surprise, Rex squinted toward the approaching pilot. The last thing he expected was the resistance of anyone, especially a woman prisoner. He watched. Vesta made her way between him and the jester prisoners; her back blocking his whip.

"Have mercy and let them be," she cried out behind her.

"Step aside, chippy," the captain demanded.

Guards surrounded Vesta. Cletus and Moe pulled her free from the jester prisoners. They dragged her back to the scrambler. Vesta noticed the guard's eyes were not as cloudy and lifeless as usual. They still jumped to the captain's every word, but they seemed different, agitated in a manner she had not noticed before.

"No," Demeter shouted. She stopped when she felt Circe's hand upon her shoulder.

Rex shoved the jester prisoners into the scrambler behind Vesta. He instructed Cletus and Moe to return the prisoners to solitary. He included the red-headed troublemaker. The warden would deal with her after the Pair Day games. He instructed them to return at once.

They sped away in a cloud of dust.

Chapter 20:
The Secrets of Tartarus

Vesta kept the stolen laser pistol from detection during the transport to the solitary confinement sector. It rested in the small of her back, secured with a tatter of cloth. After shoving the jester prisoners into their cells, Moe pushed her down the long, dark corridor of single cells. It smelled like spoiled bio-matter. The cells were tiny. She heard women behind the barred entryways. There were audible moans of dismay. Prayers to a god that had long abandoned them. A rhythmical wet thumping of a prisoner banging her head steadily against a stone wall.

"Where are you taking me?" Vesta asked.

"Does it matter?" Moe said. "If it was up to me, you'd be Pharon chow."

They stopped at the last cell at the end of the corridor. Moe slid the cell door open. It groaned along rusty tracks. He pushed Vesta inside.

Cletus stared at Vesta, aiming his weapon at her head.

Moe pulled the barred door shut. The lock refused to engage. He sighed, reaching for his keys on his belt loop to lock the cell manually. He froze. They were not there. Panic seized him. He realized he left them back in the scrambler.

He never did that. That was so unlike any of them. Rex ordered them to secure the prisoners. They could not complete that order. Nobody ever forgot their keys. Nobody ever forgot anything. It was inconceivable.

He informed Cletus of the situation.

"Stupid chippy. She's making us miss the Pair Day games. I say just leave her." His voice held inflictions not consistent with their usual robotic tone.

"Rex won't like it," Moe said. It was strange to hear his fellow guard defy a direct order. He had to admit that he agreed. If not for the chippy's insolence, he would be at the Fight Zone with everyone else.

"Rex can suck my taser," Cletus said. He stopped for a moment. Such words had never passed across his lips before. He remembered the security system did not monitor the solitary cellblock. There were no security cameras, no vid-screen recorders. No one heard but them. He felt odd. He felt, free? He continued.

"All I'm saying is that there's nowhere for her to go and we're missing all the action."

"Yeah, I've got wagers on the Pair Day games myself." Moe wanted to return to the games. The chippy's destiny was of no importance unless she fought for her life in the Fight Zone.

"Exactly. Why should we suffer for something she did?"

Moe knew this was all wrong, but he agreed with Cletus. His mind was fuzzy, but what Cletus said made sense. He decided not to go back to the scrambler to retrieve the keys. There was still the outer lock of the solitary chamber. They would still lock her in, just not in a cell.

If they left now, they would be back for more of the games to watch. A small part of him knew it was wrong, but a bigger part did not care. He looked at Vesta, who stood staring at him with her arms crossed.

"Listen up, chippy. Try anything unruly, and I promise this cell will be the last thing you ever see."

"And not your ugly puss? Do you promise?"

Moe slapped her across the face. It gave him a great thrill to feel the sting of his flesh on hers. He raised his hand to punch her, but Cletus grabbed his arm.

"C'mon, she's not worth it."

Moe's chest heaved with anger. He considered the woman a moment longer, but stood down. A bark of laughter erupted out of him as he turned to Cletus.

"Yeah, I've got money riding on the games."

They clapped each other on the back and turned to leave. Their laughter echoed throughout the corridor until the heavy metal door at the end of the corridor opened and then slammed shut behind them.

Wait, were they laughing?

What is going on with the guards?

Vesta had no time to delve into her thoughts. Her face stung, and her back ached where she landed on the stolen laser pistol. Aches inflamed her entire body. She twisted and retrieved the laser pistol. The weapon removed, she laid flat on the cell floor and let out a long sigh. She clasped her hands together and closed her eyes in prayer.

"Mother of the Many Moons, I have truly messed things up this time. Help me help Demeter and Artemis escape."

From the darkness, a voice said, "Who are Demeter and Artemis?"

Mother of the Many Moons?

Vesta sat up, squinting into the darkness. Light emitted from a dirty illumination bar affixed to the ceiling in the outer corridor. Her eyes adjusted to the darkness. She saw the outline of a woman huddled on the floor. She leaned against the wall.

"Who are Demeter and Artemis?" the woman repeated. She sounded old. She hacked to clear her throat.

"Sworn allies who are like sisters to me. Who are you?" She stood and approached the woman with caution.

"I am Eris," she said.

"Eris?" Vesta said. She recognized the name from Jeb's intel. "The former warden of this prison planet?" She sat down on the edge of the cot.

"Left for dead by Enyo, that back-stabbing bitch." The woman spat. "But not before I took her eye." She smiled. That memory always made her smile.

"I have to get out of here," Vesta said. Her words came fast. "Demeter and Artemis are depending on me. We had a plan to escape. Or… we had a plan until I got thrown in here."

Eris said, "Maybe you can pray to the Mother of the Many Moons again."

"Yeah." Vesta was losing her patience. She had to get out of the solitary confinement block. They were depending on her to fly them off of this rock.

"She provides," Eris said. "She does."

The old woman leaned forward. She shoved a shiv into the pilot's hand. Vesta scooted away on the cot.

"Hey!"

"Oh, it's not for you." Eris moved to her right. A whoosh of stale air flowed into the cell from an open vent in the cell wall. The old woman blocked the vent with her body when the guards had approached.

"I've been unscrewing this sucker and trying to widen the opening."

"Say no more," Vesta said.

She retrieved the laser pistol.

"I think we can speed things up." She set the pistol to its highest setting.

Chapter 21:
Sister Battles Sister

The prisoners stood under the watchful eye of the guards. Since Vesta's outburst, the guards kept their sidearms handy.

Demeter noted their strange behavior. They expressed their agitation over the simplest commands. They wanted only to watch the battles. A couple lowered their laser pistols because the day was hot, and their arms grew tired. One even dared make the comment that Enyo wouldn't be half bad looking if she would drop the attitude.

Demeter studied them. Their eyes seemed more alert than usual, less like they were in a zombie trance. Circe approached her.

"What was Vesta thinking?" Circe said. "She's the pilot. She has the weapon!"

"A hiccup. We will be fine." Demeter did not take her attention off the guards.

"A hiccup! Really? Do you mean that if the guards kill her, a corpse is going to fly us out of here?" Circe's voice rose as she spoke.

"Have you noticed the guards today? It's like…" Circe didn't let her finish the thought. She stared at Demeter.

"And let me remind you. If Vesta is out of the picture, I swore loyalty to her, not you."

Enyo approached the vid-screen. The spectators responded with cheers.

"Now, my Lords and Ladies, time for today's match."

"It had better be good. I lost money last time!" a voice from the crowd yelled out. Others laughed and heckled the unlucky speaker.

"It will be good," Enyo said. Her voice boomed. She smirked. "It will be spectacular. Guards, bring out the Pair Day challengers!"

The guards marched the prisoners from the other cellblock onto the Fight Zone. They appeared from behind the giant vid-screen. Artemis and Leda led the new prisoners.

As the women marched into the center of the Fight Zone, catcalls and whoops erupted from the dais.

Artemis!

They must have stayed behind on the Palamino until the games began.

After the ruckus with Vesta, the guards corralled Demeter and the others closer to the scramblers. They never noticed when the new prisoners marched from the transport ship.

There was a restless clicking behind her. The Pharon circled the interior of the covered cargo cage. The crowd was more geared up and boisterous today, which agitated the beast.

"Don't allow these pleasing faces to fool you," Enyo said. She held the smirk. "These are hardened criminals. They will fight hand to hand with their rival cellblock."

Enyo strolled toward Artemis. She brushed her chin upward with her robotic hand. The chill of cold, dead metal made the girl's flesh prickle. The cyber-eye scanned her face.

Rex made the slightest move to intervene, then thought better of it. In the still desert air, he heard the sniggering of one of his guards behind him. Another made the comment, "Looks like the warden is moving in on El Capitan's chippy." His temples throbbed with rage, but he remained where he stood.

"First to do battle is this one," Enyo announced. She traced one robotic fingertip down the unblemished cheek of the young woman and locked her eyes on the girl's. "What is your name?"

"Artemis," she said. She averted her eyes to the sand.

"Speak up, prisoner," the warden said.

"Artemis!" Her voice boomed with unexpected resonance. A quiet enveloped the spectators. "Named after the goddess of the twin moons."

Enyo laughed. She had not expected a flower of such delicate appearance to possess such prickly thorns.

"Artemis, a goddess," Enyo announced. Her tone was one of amusement. She turned to the prisoners from the opposing cellblock. "And she will do battle with... that one."

The robotic hand picked out Demeter in the line-up.

Circe gripped Demeter's arm, but the warrior pulled away from her.

"You can't," Circe whispered. *This wasn't part of the plan.*

Demeter stepped forward, bowing before Enyo.

"I am Demeter. It is my honor to fight on Pair Day."

Artemis's eyes filled with surprise, then narrowed. Her sister had arrived to rescue her. Again. The flames of resentment spread quickly.

Circe clenched her hands into fists. "I should have known better than to trust a bounty hunter." She kicked at the sand.

Demeter sauntered over to Artemis, looking her up and down. She did this for the benefit of the cheering crowd. She made a face of complete disgust, and they cheered more.

Conflicting emotions thundered through Artemis. The relief she should have felt was all but gone. Demeter had come for her, but the overriding emotion was anger, not relief. That was also because Demeter had come for her.

Pushing those emotions down, she recognized something in her big sister's eyes and knew the plan.

"Step back, chippy," Enyo said. Her cyber-eye tracked Demeter's every move.

"I only want to be certain this prisoner is ready for a proper fight. Are you ready for this, *sister*?" Laced with faux poison, her words rousted the spectators. Unknown to the rowdy crowd, the warrior was speaking two languages simultaneously.

Circe heard it. It was the tone in which Demeter said *sister*. She now understood what was unfolding before her.

"You're scaring me," Artemis said in a childish voice, but the slightest pinch of sarcasm cut through. The spectators cheered too ecstatically to notice.

Demeter laughed and circled Artemis, continuing to size her up. Enyo stood back. She watched how this played out.

"I'm scaring her," Demeter called out, playing to the spectators on the giant screen. "And not one blow landed. Your guests deserve more. This child is unfit for battle."

At once, the spectators booed and hissed. They were unhappy with the warrior's decision not to destroy her chosen opponent.

Enyo snatched Demeter's arm and spun the warrior around, so they were face to face.

"You're becoming a real pain in my ass, ghost of Tacitus."

"Let me make amends, warden." Demeter turned to face the spectators. "I propose a better fight," she exclaimed.

The warden was losing what little patience she had. The auburn-haired warrior was commandeering her wager games.

"Spit it out," Enyo said.

Demeter smiled and waited a moment longer before she said, "Battle Elite."

The cyber-eye focused on the warrior with a buzzing whirl.

"What are you trying to pull?"

"Pit me against Circe. She's your best fighter. And I'm the only one of her equal. A really unruly fight. That's what your esteemed spectators want to see."

"And what else?" Enyo asked, the brow of her real eye rose suspiciously. She could tell her spectators were not enjoying this exchange between her and the warrior prisoner. They wanted action, not words.

"And I have a score to settle with Circe. What say you?"

Enyo glanced from Demeter to the spectators. Many grew restless. Some threatened to leave before the games even began. She spun on her heels toward the screen and exclaimed, "Battle Elite! The best fighters compete!"

The spectators rose to their feet, cheering wildly. Enyo seized the moment and shouted, "Demeter against Circe! Chippy against chippy! The most bloody, vicious battle of them all!"

Another thunder of approval erupted from the dais.

"No!"

All eyes turned to Artemis. The video-drones projected her face upon the big screen. Her lips formed a feral snarl.

"What?" Enyo asked, amused.

"You paired us, your wardenship, so I am honor bound to fight this one who calls me *sister*."

What is she doing? She's messing everything up!

Demeter's mind tried rationalizing why Artemis would do this. This was not the place for her childlike rebellion.

It took all the discipline she had for Demeter not to look shocked at her sister's outburst. Inside, she wanted to grab her sister and shake her.

Taunting Artemis, Enyo said, "I thought you feared the warrior, little one." Her words teased the girl, and the crowd approved.

"I am not scared of this woman who acts like a warrior." Artemis regarded Demeter with a dismissive glance. "She believes she is the strongest, the smartest. I say she is nothing more than a bully. I say she does nothing more than try to control everything and everyone around her."

Artemis, please shut up!

Enyo gave Rex a confused glance. The big captain shrugged his shoulders.

"You are but a child," Demeter cried out. "Not fit to combat one such as I."

Artemis glared at her.

"I am not a child!" Her words were as ferocious as any Pharon shriek.

"You are a child. A dumb, silly child who has no experience worth anything. You can't even take care of yourself." Demeter played the crowd. "You are obviously incapable of making moral decisions. Being exiled to Prison Planet is proof of that."

The crowd cheered, and the wagering began.

"For your information, I don't know why I'm here. The best I can tell, I was unruly. Yeah, I'm unruly! No different from yourself."

Demeter bit her tongue. She put everything on the line to save her baby sister and Artemis was nothing more than a spoiled brat deserving of…

Artemis bolted toward her, arms outstretched. Before Demeter reacted, she felt her body pushed backwards. She landed on her butt. A puff of dust billowed from under her, and the crowd cheered.

"That was for Sandor," Artemis said for only Demeter's ears to hear. She kicked sand at Demeter for good measure.

Regret punched Demeter in the gut.

Damn! she thought, wiping sand from her legs and gown. *It was about Parbola. It was always about Parbola. I ruined everything for her with Sandor.*

"So, the goddess proves to be as ferocious as the Pharon, with a bite as big as her shriek," Enyo said. The crowd approved.

Demeter found her feet. Her sister began jabbing her with her pointy fingers.

"You never know when to give up, do you?" Artemis spoke between jabs.

Demeter slapped her hand away, deflecting the jabs.

"I'm here to save you," Demeter said silently through gritted teeth so the video-drones did not reveal her words.

"I don't need to be saved." It was a lie, but Artemis said it anyway.

"I dropped everything as soon as I heard you disappeared," Demeter said. "Do you understand, Artemis? Everything!"

"What do you want? Valor medals? A hero's parade? Famous bounty hunter to rescue little sister once again." She continued jabbing.

"You don't seem as if you wanted me to bother." Demeter grew angrier with each sharp jab.

The video-drones followed as the women circled each other. Every time Artemis jabbed Demeter, the crowd cheered.

"Of course, I wanted you to save me," Artemis said. "I even prayed for it. But when I saw you, I realized how mad I still am at you. That anger hasn't changed, it hasn't gone away."

"That's fine. You can be angry with me after we get off of this rock."

"No!"

Artemis lashed out, throwing everything she had into the effort, and pushed Demeter onto her backside.

"The little goddess strikes again," Enyo announced. "That is two times, warrior. Should she put you down a third time, she will be our new champion and you will provide dinner for the Pharon."

Pulse racing, anger swelling, Demeter leaped to her feet. She had to end this before serious harm came to Artemis.

"I am so sick of you always telling me what to do," Artemis said. She continued jabbing Demeter. "You never stop. You never stop trying to get me to be like you, but I'm not like you. I don't want to be like you, and I can't stand you."

Demeter swatted the hand away, then caught Artemis on the jaw with a solid right hook. It wasn't enough to knock her unconscious, but it was enough to end this squabble for the time being.

The slightest pang of regret cut through Demeter. She watched her baby sister hit the sand. It was the last thing she wanted to do. Although…

Being honest with herself and herself alone, Demeter delighted in the opportunity to knock Artemis on her ass. After the legal grief on Parbola, punching her baby sister felt kind of therapeutic.

The crowd roared. Demeter spun on her heels and returned to the line with the other prisoners. Even the guards cheered.

Rex shouted at them to stand down, but they refused to follow his commands. One of them, it might have been Cletus, mumbled for him to sit on a laser pistol and spin.

Back in Eris's cell, Vesta shaved off another sliver of metal and stone. The laser beam glowed red. She wiped sweat from her forehead. The vent hole was almost wide enough for them to crawl through.

She looked at Eris.

"I think I've got the hang of it now."

The old woman gave her an approving smile.

Vesta went back to work, widening the last part of the vent opening.

Chapter 22:
Beneath Tartarus

Tycho and Neander rushed toward Demeter. They grabbed her arms and escorted her the rest of the way to the lineup. The guards were putting on a show for their captain, but Demeter noticed they were less rough than usual. In fact, she would have sworn that Tycho was rubbing her upper arm tenderly with his thumb.

What is going on with these creeps?

They shoved her toward the others, but not as forcefully as expected. Circe stared in silence. She turned and watched Cletus and Moe escort Artemis out of the Fight Zone.

Artemis rubbed her jaw. The guards led her to the scrambler. They secured her in the back until they could transport her to the prison sick bay for the Biotron Medi-droid to examine her vitals. The sisters shared a glance. Fleeting as it was, that one look conveyed fear, anger, concern, regret, forgiveness, and love.

Pain aside, Artemis shed a tear of joy, knowing she wasn't alone. No matter where she went, she had a stupid big sister. Demeter loved her to the end of the galaxy and back.

We're getting out of here.

No words passed between the sisters. Just a simple glance that said everything.

"Stand back. One last blast," Vesta said. She braced herself for the kickback, let out a breath, and fired.

A brilliant flash of red light emitted from the business end of the laser pistol. The last layer of rock vanished. It burned bright red for a moment, then the edge of the rock cooled. Smoke filled the air.

Vesta peered into the tunnel.

"Where does this go?"

"To the perimeter of the Fight Zone, where we can disrupt the force-shield," she said.

"I have to tell you, Eris, I have a promise to keep. I have to rescue my friends." She secured the weapon with the tattered ribbon of fabric around her waist.

"And I made a promise to get out of this hellhole." The old woman's words were dry.

Vesta peered into the tunnel again and said, "Tight fit." Her voice echoed in the foreboding darkness.

"No problem. I'll go first."

The old woman used her bony hand to push Vesta out of the way.

Vesta admired Eris. The former warden had been to hell and back. She never lost hope of escaping this place. Even surrounded by darkness, the woman clung to the light.

I have to respect that.

Vesta followed Eris into the tunnel and tried to keep up.

Eyes shut tightly to the darkness; Vesta imagined the woman in front of her. She imagined her form, listened to her movements. The clap of her palms atop the stone floor, the shuffle of her knees. She smelled her, the ground under them and the damp stone above. Demeter taught her this. Perceive the world with your senses, not just your eyes.

She blocked out all the other sounds around them, honing in on only the sounds Eris made. Vesta blocked out the echoing drip of liquid. The scuttle of tiny legs over rocks. The slither of another creature across sand.

When it sounded like the old woman was lengthening her body to fit through a narrow passage, Vesta followed. Her back scraped the tunnel ceiling. She ignored it, ignored the tons of granite, rock, and sand above her. She rejected the notion the world above would crush her flat if the vent tunnel gave way.

In her mind's eye, she imagined following the woman into a wide expanse of openness. By not focusing on the narrow tunnel helped keep her breathing normal. There was nothing to fear.

"I see a light," Eris said with a huff. Her pace over the rocks never slackened.

Sweat covered Vesta's face and back. Her entire body felt slick and dirty. She dared not open her eyes. Not yet. It was better to keep her senses on high alert.

Eris moved swiftly through the dark corridors. She moved with purpose, like her life depended on it.

When Vesta opened her eyes, they were crawling into an open section of the tunnel. The chamber was lofty enough to allow them to stand and brush rocks from their hands and knees.

They moved quick, following the light, until they came to the last narrow stretch of the passage.

Chapter 23:
The Ghost of Tacitus

Circe and Demeter faced off in the Fight Zone. Guards surrounded them. Laser pistols were half-heartedly aimed in their general direction. Demeter struggled to understand what was going on with them when Circe spoke.

"I hope you know what you're doing, bounty hunter."

The video-drones buzzed the air around the combatants. High-speed lenses profiled each fighter for the benefit of the spectators. Enyo observed the numbers on the comm-tracker rise. Mega-credit vouchers changed hands at a frantic pace. Demeter heard the chatter from the spectators. They wagered thousands of credits on Circe. Others took the bets and raised the stakes in favor of the "warrior with the mane of fire." Still others wagered on which of the fighters would suffer the bloodiest demise.

Rex barked a command for the guards to step aside. He entered the Fight Zone brandishing blue and red ribbons. He caught the agitated look Moe directed at him. The guard hesitated a moment. When he finally stepped aside, Moe spit in the sand, watching the captain enter the Fight Zone with contempt in his gaze.

Even Enyo noticed. Thankfully, the spectators focused on placing wagers and not the guard's insubordination.

I've never seen this behavior before.

Her thought trailed away. The cyber-eye scanned and whirled, focusing on the guards. She scanned one to the other. They looked different. It was in their eyes.

Their eyes!

"Bat-tles! Bat-tles! Bat-tles!"

The roar from the royal dais shook her back into the moment.

She nodded to Rex to proceed. The captain moved to the line where Circe stood and handed her the red ribbon. She took and tied it around one bare arm. The other he gave to Demeter.

Demeter tied the ribbon to her arm when the captain leaned in close and said, "The Pharons will feast on pretty meals tonight." He chuckled and called for his guards to exit the Fight Zone.

Enyo stepped between the two warriors. Peering into the giant vid-screen, she soaked in the expectant faces. She raised her arms for attention. "My Lords and Ladies, prepare yourselves for a historic Pair Day! Blood-thirsty unrulies will battle to the death, by hand or by blade, to the bitter end!"

Hundreds of voices all cried out in one jubilant cheer.

Enyo raised two flags. One was red, and the other was blue.

"At the drop of these pennants, let combat begin!"

Before the pennants fell, Demeter crossed the line and approached Circe. They spoke, then ran to the side, huddling with the other prisoners.

A silent confusion fell over the spectators.

Not again, ghost of Tacitus!

Enyo frowned. The warden had grown weary of the warrior's antics in the Fight Zone.

Enyo nodded to Rex to find out what the prisoners were doing. The guards were the only ones making any noise. They jeered, yelling at the fighters to continue the bout.

He marched to where the prisoners stood. "What's going on?" His tone was gruff.

"We need to plan our strategy," Demeter said.

"You want a good show for your spectators, don't you?" Circe added.

Rex grunted his approval, cracking his whip for effect. That was enough to nudge the crowd out of their stupor and get them whooping again.

"Bat-tles! Bat-tles! Bat-tles!"

Demeter talked quickly, regarding each woman as she relayed the plan one last time. "We have to make this look good, a real rabble-rouser, but no kills."

She stared in Circe's direction.

"Do you understand?"

Circe snarled and then smirked. "You take all the fun out of everything."

The huddle broke and Demeter and Circe returned to the Fight Zone. Each combatant had their arm with the ribbon tied to it raised.

"For the red!" Circe cried.

"For the blue!" Demeter said.

"Finally," Enyo mumbled under her breath. She raised the pennants.

"Let's get ready for Battle Elite!"

Vesta continued wiggling through the tunnel behind Eris. It was a tight fit, even for her slender figure.

"How much further?" the pilot asked. She suffered from claustrophobia and tight spaces made her nauseous. She focused on the image in her mind of the woman in front of her, walking upright in a vast cavern. The rough surface of the rock ceiling scraping her back constantly broke her concentration.

"Close enough to freedom I can taste it," the old woman replied.

Vesta made a sour face.

"I'm tasting something in here too, but it's not freedom."

"Come on, girlie," Eris said with a smile. She continued scurrying forward.

Chapter 24: Clash of the Warriors

Enyo held the pennants high. The crowd counted down.

"Three, two, one…"

When the gong rang out, Enyo dropped both pennants. They hit the sand.

Circe and Demeter hurled themselves at one other. Their war cries sounded like the Dogen banshee howling in the endless night of the Lambda Zone.

Their bodies crashed head-on, locking in deadly combat. The spectators jumped to their feet, shouting, and cheering.

The warrior women fell onto the hot sand, bodies rolling. Body over body, the colored ribbons spinning in the whipping flurry of auburn and raven hair. When they stopped, Demeter took the dominant top position.

Below, Circe landed a jab onto Demeter's jaw. The bounty hunter retaliated with a body blow to Circe's midsection that emptied her lungs of air.

Circe rolled out from under Demeter, grabbing her stomach. She gasped for air while the bounty hunter yelled a war cry into the buzzing video-drone zooming around her. Her demented visage filled the giant vid-screen, and the crowd loved it.

Demeter was too busy playing to the video-drone to notice Circe get to her feet and charge her from behind. She smashed Demeter full in the back and sent her crashing down. The audience could not get enough.

I hope you kill each other, the warden thought. She checked the wager counter. Bets continued pouring in.

Enyo watched the women battle, then turned her attention back to the guards. They were whooping and hollering with the best of them. Rex yelled at them to pipe down, but none paid him any heed.

It was a flagrant act of insubordination she had never seen during her time as warden.

The combatants squared off, circling the Fight Zone with little hops and jumps on the balls of their feet. Before anyone could accuse the fighters of stalling, Demeter moved with the speed of the stars. She snatched free the flimsy gown from Circe, revealing a muscular body that displayed the most extravagant tattoos from across the universe. Dirty undergarments were the only scraps of fabric that remained.

The crowd roared with joyous glee. The wager counter jumped again. Enyo watched the numbers rise on her comm-tracker, doubling and then tripling.

Circe reciprocated, tearing the flimsy garment off of Demeter. She exposed the warrior's trim, muscular physique to all. Similar dirty undergarments covered her most delicate places.

Enraged, Demeter lunged at Circe and dragged her to the sand. They rolled over one another. They pulled hair and tried choking each other. Cheers filled the air above the constant whoosh of the airborne video-drones filming the action.

"This is your plan?" Circe asked. The upper hand was hers. She rolled on top and held Demeter's arms over her head. She quickly tried to catch her breath.

"This is a distraction," Demeter said. Her breathing was also heavy, coming out in gasps. "So, we can make our way to the transport ship. But we have to take out the force-shield projector so we can pass."

Circe punched Demeter in the jaw to jubilant adulation from the spectators.

"What was that for?" Demeter asked. Anger filled her words.

"We gotta make it look real," Circe smirked.

"Well done," Demeter said.

"Thanks."

Demeter bolted upright and head-butted Circe. White light flashed before her eyes, and she slid off Demeter, crumbling to the ground, holding her face in both hands.

At the farthest perimeter edge of the Fight Zone, a wire vent cover in a jutting rock formation rattled. It rattled a second time and then a third. The fourth time Vesta kicked it, it popped free from its fasteners and fell away from the vent opening.

Vesta and Eris emerged from the vent. Sun light temporarily blinded them after their long crawl through darkness. Filth and sweat covered their bodies.

Almost at once Vesta heard the cheering from the dais projected onto the vid-screen. In the distance she saw two women, one tall with red hair and the other shorter and covered in tattoos, fighting furiously in their underwear.

Oh no, it's started!

Vesta turned to the old woman.

"I have to rescue my friends."

Eris grabbed Vesta with more strength than expected from one so weathered and spun her around.

"Give me your laser pistol."

Vesta felt Eris's withered hand on her bare back. The wrinkly, dry flesh patted against her skin. The old woman tried tearing the pistol free from the ribbon of cloth.

Vesta struggled. She understood this was the moment Eris had been envisioning for years, but it did nothing to help her own current dilemma. She couldn't give up the laser pistol just yet.

"I need it to take down the force-shield," Vesta said, struggling against Eris. "We had a deal!"

Eris stopped. The old woman looked exhausted, but her eyes were still aglow with a desire for vengeance.

"You're right," Eris said in a rough tone. "The force-shield first."

The old woman put a hand on Vesta's shoulder, her pledge of loyalty until the force-shield crumbled. After that, she had her own destiny to follow.

Vesta retrieved the laser pistol from the ribbon around her waist and set it to its highest setting.

"Better hurry. Your friends might not last too long."

Nodding, Vesta made her way to the force-shield projector. On high alert, she moved cautiously, careful not to step too close to the energy beams and buy herself a ticket to instantaneous annihilation.

Chapter 25:
The Destruction of Tartarus

The battle between Circe and Demeter weaned. They circled, jabbed, and swung at each other.

Restlessness gnawed at the spectators. They desired action and blood. They demanded an extravaganza of death.

Enyo turned to Rex. The antics of the guards agitated him. He watched them.

"We need to ramp up the action," Enyo said. She could not hide her disgust.

"The guards…"

"I don't care about the guards," Enyo snapped, cutting the captain off.

"More blood!" someone shouted, which resulted in more chants.

Rex nodded. Mouth shut, he skulked off, head lowered. The gong sounded, and the combatants went to opposite sides of the Fight Zone. Both gasped to catch their breath.

"Rex, do this. Rex, do that," the captain said, grumbling under his breath. He spat and imagined he could hear the wad of phlegm hiss atop the hot sand. He wiped his sweaty crown with an enormous hand, stomping toward Enyo's scrambler.

Enyo kept everyone awake all night insisting how important this Pair Day was, how dire it was to regain the faith of Her Eminence. Techs pulled double shifts, some triple, brainstorming bigger entertainments for the masses. They made clown collars. Guards found the worst dregs in the solitary cells, beating them to prepare them for the festivities. No one rested.

Even when some were ready to drop, the warden continued pushing them.

Early that morning, Rex ordered Tycho to cage the Pharon in the cargo scrambler. Tycho transported the adult creature out to the Fight Zone hours before anyone else arrived. Enyo ordered him not to feed the beast. Enyo then directed the other guards to collar and chain the two Pharon younglings and prepare the smaller beasts for transport. They had a time not only getting the beasts out of their cave but also loading them onto the Palamino. For younglings, each weighed over eleven hundred kilos and could drag six strong men with little effort.

All this at Enyo's constant insistence that they produce quicker results with less sleep. Rex, like everyone else, lost track of time.

First it was evening. Then it was the dead of night. Finally, it was dawn. He lost track of everything, and it resulted in the guards missing their Kapitron injections.

Over time, they grew a tolerance to the drug's effects. Daily injections were of the utmost importance to ensure their obedience. Kapitron not only kept them submissive, but also curbed any desires they felt toward the female inmates. It prevented them from acting out their every savage impulse. It ensured their docility.

They were becoming belligerent. Rex watched how they managed the prisoners. The guards did not oversee them as instructed. Their looks lingered. They began touching. From the moment they began their service to the Prison Planet, they barely noticed the women. For most, it was the first time they had touched a woman in any other manner than to grab and shove them to satisfy an order.

He threw the back hatch open. Surprised, he saw Artemis curled in a ball in one corner.

Those dummies put the prisoner in the wrong scrambler!

The girl looked less frightened and more concerned with what was going on outside the scrambler.

"Who is winning the battle?" she asked in a rush of words.

"Worry not about such matters that do not concern you, chippy," the captain said. He had no time for the lovely creature. He located the locked box Enyo sent him to retrieve. Without another word, he squeezed the black box to his chest and slammed the scrambler door shut.

This could be bad, Rex thought.

What could result from the guards missing just one injection?

He marched toward the combatants. A video-drone followed him. Cheering erupted from the dais. They knew what the black box contained.

Shards of red and blue ribbon, and garments of cloth, littered the Fight Zone. Each fighter strained to control their breathing. Cuts oozing blood and fresh bruises covered their bodies. The tall warrior's cheek was red. Four long furrows inflamed her flesh.

Demeter tried reading the captain's face. Deep thoughts were going on underneath that bald, sun scorched cranium.

Rex pushed a code into the lock, snapped it open. The crowd applauded wildly when the reflection of multiple suns glinted off the laser knife hafts in the box. Enyo removed the knives. More approving applause. They sparked to life. She held them both in the robotic hand.

With expert precision, the robotic hand flicked twice. Both blades sliced into the sand at the feet of each fighter. The laser blades cut into the sand with such intense heat, the sand sizzled and began transforming the granules into tiny glass particles.

"Come to mama," Circe said. She scooped the blade from the sand.

"Very nice," Demeter said. She admired the laser blade's craftsmanship.

The gong rang, a new thunder of excitement erupted among the spectators. Before the combatants charged into battle, the world shook beneath them.

An explosion of fire and sparks blasted out. A plume of thick black smoke followed, staining the blue sky. Another explosion rocked the Fight Zone, and the workings inside the metal casing of the force-shield projector detonated in a violent flash of fire and smoke.

Fire engulfed the force-shield projector at the far end of the Fight Zone. Moments later, another explosion disrupted the stillness adjacent from the blazing projector. The ground reverberated. A chain reaction explosion reached the next projector.

The force-shield broke into visible static until blinking out like a faulty vid-screen.

The video-drones could not predict the next point of destruction as the sequence of explosions continued shaking the ground. They buzzed overhead, covering every moment for the jubilant masses.

None of the spectators on the dais understood what transpired. They just reacted. It was a spectacle. It was entertainment.

The ground rumbled and the giant vid-screen vibrated from the shock waves.

The third projector, the one opposite the corralled prisoners, detonated in a deafening burst of sparks and fire. The women screamed and ran for cover. More of the black smoke coughed into the air. Fire reached high into the blue sky.

"What was that?" Circe asked after the third projector exploded.

"My guess is an unruly Vesta," Demeter said over the ruckus. She could not hold back her smile.

The spectators on the vid-screen cheered. Enyo acted like it was all part of the entertainment. She had promised them something special.

"Guards!" Rex shouted. They appeared scared, like the prisoners. Except for Cletus, who giggled and grabbed at the women, the rest ran away from the flames.

The third explosion riled the Pharon. She shrieked, thrashing about in the cargo cage. Her giant, whipping body smashed into the walls of the cage, and the scrambler teetered from side to side.

After the last projector exploded, a devastating blast of fire and smoke engulfed the day. Everyone ran for cover. The very surface of the planet was alive with flames. Hot clouds of black smoke and debris choked out the blistering light from the multiple suns. The giant vid-screen went blank. Except for the vibrations from the last explosion, the world was quiet.

The shock waves shook the video-drones from their flight paths. Each exploded onto the sandy, barren terrain.

It was a living hell of fire, smoke, and silence.

"I didn't expect that," Vesta said. Her voice was tiny. Her ears rang.

"What did you expect it to do, fart once and roll over dead?" Eris asked.

Vesta snatched a nearby rock. She tossed it toward the force-shield. It passed without resistance.

No sizzle. No zap.

Vesta smiled at Eris. The old woman held out a weathered palm.

"Hand it over," she said. She sounded revitalized, no longer tired. Adrenaline pumped through Eris.

The laser pistol slapped into the old woman's brittle palm. She glanced through the settling dust toward the prison.

"I need to help my people now," Vesta said.

"I hope you make it, but I hope Enyo doesn't."

The women exchanged one last look. The old woman winked at Vesta before running off into a nearby rock formation. Another hidden tunnel entrance.

The sound of the laser weapon rang out.

May the Mother of Many Moons help anyone stupid enough to get in her way.

The former warden knew the entire layout of the tunnel system beneath the prison. She knew every darkened corridor and passageway.

Vesta ran toward the Fight Zone.

Chapter 26:
Revolt of the Captive Women

"The force-shield is down!" Demeter exclaimed.

Bodies crawled through the debris.

A loud metallic ripping followed a savage crunch of metal. The scrambler containing the cargo cage flipped to one side. The Pharon used her claws to slice open the top of the cage. She forced her body through. The pointed tail whipping wildly, it smashed into Enyo's nearby transport scrambler.

The warden's scrambler rolled end over end, ceasing only when it crashed into the prisoner scrambler. It rolled to a stop on its roof. It shook Artemis violently inside. Her body slammed into the side, floor, side, roof and again until it stopped.

When the scrambler finished moving, she tried collecting her bearings. Her head spun, and she felt disoriented. Everything hurt. Demeter's uppercut was nothing compared to the fresh aches and pains throbbing throughout her body. She looked around and realized a blast of light cut into the transport.

The scrambler's back door ripped free from its hinges in the tumble.

She crawled toward the light.

Outside, the world was hot and still. Bolts of dusty sunlight blasted through the thick cloud of smoke covering the Fight Zone.

Artemis stood. Her right shoulder throbbed. Unsure whether she could even raise her arm, she looked around. The smoke and dust limited her visibility. She heard voices calling out.

It was impossible to tell whether the figure standing a couple of feet from her was friend or foe.

She was about to call out when rough hands grabbed her. They threw her against the side of the overturned scrambler.

Artemis cried out in pain.

"Where you are going, chippy?" Tycho leanded into her, pushing her body into the tattered vehichle. He appeared insane. "Hot date with old fat Rex? Forget him, chippy. I'm a real man." He smiled. Artemis tried pushing him away, but he clasped her wrists. He laughed, pressing his body into hers.

She squirmed. Pain erupted up her arms when Tycho squeezed her wrists together. The strain on her injured shoulder made her wince and tear up.

A savage shriek pierced the air. From the swirling cloud of dust and smoke, the Pharon stomped across the sand. She studied the puny creatures below. She recognized the one that constantly antagonized her with weapons and words.

Anger filled the Pharon's eyes. The beast snorted. Her brows arched.

"I'll take care of you," Tycho yelled at the Pharon. He fought to free his laser pistol. He was not quicker than the beast.

The scorpion tail struck. The pointed end exploded through Tycho's midsection, lifting him before he realized what was happening. He stared stupidly at the tail protruding from his chest.

The Pharon swung him around. Artemis saw his face pale. Gouts of blood poured from the wound in his chest. Undaunted, he fumbled to retrieve the laser pistol until he dropped it.

An agonized scream tore from Tycho's lungs. The beast shrieked. With a vicious flick of her tail, the Pharon sliced Tycho's body in half. Each half flying in the opposite direction, flung far into the distant, sweltering wasteland.

His scream echoed for a moment. Then the only sound he made was the wet splat of his mangled, tattered halves splattering the jutting rock formations and desert terrain.

The beast shrieked again, this time for her younglings. They took her away from them so early in the morning. She was determined to find them.

"Thank you," a tiny voice called out.

The Pharon looked down and observed the other creature, the one her tormentor had been terrorizing. She recognized a kindred spirit in this tiny creature. The creature was a prisoner in this place, just like she and her younglings.

"Thank you," Artemis said again, louder. If she had learned anything from her years traveling the galaxy, it was the code of gratitude. It paid to remember to always thank the universe for every kindness it gifted you.

The Pharon shrieked, responding to Artemis's words. The beast lowered her head and nudged the little creature onto her neck. There was no telling who this youngling belonged to, but the Pharon felt a motherly duty to protect it.

Artemis knew she had to find Demeter, knew they had to get out of here, but there was no way she was going to pass up the opportunity to ride on a Pharon!

Bars of sunlight broke through the thick clouds. Circe saw the outline of a giant beast emerging from the dust.

"Look!"

Like a mythical beast traversing from one magical dimension into another, the Pharon stepped from the swirling dust and smoke with heavy steps. Atop her neck sat Artemis, perched like a warrior woman ready for battle.

"Demeter!" she yelled and waved a hand over her head.

"Looks like this is going to be a Pair Day for the books," Circe said with a smirk.

"Artemis," Demeter shouted up to her.

The beast stopped before the other creatures. Artemis slid down the Pharon's scaly, hairy neck when the beast lowered her head. She ran to Demeter, and the sisters embraced.

Relief flooded through Demeter.

"Get the prisoners back to their cells," Enyo demanded. "Now!"

Rex lost track of his guards in the chaos. Dust continued settling. He witnessed the prisoners overpowering his guards, beating them with their own weapons.

"Oh, crap."

More guards rushed from the edge of the dust cloud. The prisoners from both cellblocks overpowered them. They fought like wild women, using whatever they found as a weapon. In the absence of any instrument of destruction, they used their teeth and hands.

Rex saw Neander and Moe in the fray. He noticed that they had drawn their laser pistols, but they didn't respond fast enough. They hesitated. That moment of hesitation cost both men their lives.

Neander fell screaming onto Prison Planet's hot surface. The prisoners swarmed him like hungry Blue Star beetles. He struggled, but they suppressed his escape. A prisoner with a bright purple mohawk gripped a laser blade and buried it deep into Neander's tender throat. His scream ended in a sharp, choking sizzle of flesh and blood. Moe screamed, tried pulling away from the women, but they held him tight. He pleaded with them. He screamed for mercy.

Using their bare hands, they rendered him into little more than a human sized broken doll.

Rex watched. The women beat the men to their knees. They were ferocious. The Pharon slaughtered more guards. It was a massacre.

Without the Kapitron coursing through their brains, they were unsure what to do. Their trained survival instincts dulled; they questioned their actions. They needed a command to return everything to normal. That command would never come. They were no longer the superior force keeping the unruly prisoners in line.

Leda led the women with a howl. When a guard grabbed her, she smacked him on the nose with the golden hairbrush. He screamed. She tugged the helmet from his head and beat him with the brush until he collapsed.

Vesta entered the Fight Zone, her war cry piercing the air.

Chapter 27:
The End of the World

In the watchtower, Zorn awoke with a start. Earlier he convinced Ordric to accompany Enyo for the Pair Day events. As soon as the warden was gone, Zorn fell asleep. It was a rare moment of peace he enjoyed, knowing the insane, one-eyed chippy wasn't anywhere near him.

After the previous night, he slept soundly; he doubted the end of the world would awaken him. He rubbed the crust from the corners of his eyes and yawned.

The tech wondered about the wager games. He switched on the vid-screen covering the Fight Zone. A tumbler filled with the warden's finest scotch sat on the console. He retrieved it and sipped. She would never know. Besides, it would be easy enough to point blame at Rex if she suspected anything.

The screen blinked to life.

"Let's see how Pair Day goes."

He took another sip but spit it out when the vid-screen blinked to life. The tumbler slammed atop the console. Zorn sat bolt upright in his chair.

Was it the end of the world?

The Fight Zone was a war zone. Prisoners overpowered the

guards. The four force-shield projectors burned, flames reaching into the sky. Black smoke filled the air.

Eyes darted from the vid-screen to the destruction outside. Black clouds stained the distant sky over the Fight Zone like an ugly bruise.

Zorn pushed buttons and flipped toggles, but there were no transmissions from the video-drones.

He used the joystick to direct the observation camera atop the watchtower. Zorn zoomed in, focusing on the Fight Zone. Enyo shouted commands. The Pharon was loose! It struck down guards with that deadly tail, slashing them to shreds. The creature did not slow its assault.

"I'm out of here." He rose.

Without haste, Zorn gathered documents, files, and info-cassettes, anything incriminating, all he could carry. Stuffing materials into his coat pockets, he raced out of the watchtower. He had to reach the escape capsules. There were a limited number and Zorn was the only tech with all the codes. Enyo didn't have all the escape codes.

He pressed the button to summon the elevator.

"C'mon," he said, jabbing the button repeatedly.

The doors opened leisurely once the car arrived. He rushed inside, pushing the *down* button furiously. The doors whooshed shut, and the car began its slow descent.

Zorn did not wonder what transpired out at the Fight Zone. He didn't care. It was Enyo and Rex's mess. They created the games after overthrowing Eris, turning the prisoners into gladiators. They paid the Space Service to bring them prisoners on false charges, and they alone deserved to burn for what they did.

Zorn fleetingly thought about returning to the watchtower. The computer and remaining info-cassettes needed to be destroyed. He decided against it. The car reached the bottom of its descent.

The doors whooshed open. A wave of savage-faced prisoners flooded the car. Hands holding tools from the tool shed grabbed at him. He screamed, fear choking him. Desperate hands pulled him to the floor. Nails raked his flesh. The tools transformed into weapons in the hands of the released inmates.

"We are all unruly," they howled. They ripped him to pieces.

Vesta and Demeter hooked elbows. They pivoted together, using the momentum to land punches on two advancing guards.

They sprang apart.

"The force-shield is down!" Vesta said.

"Good job," Demeter said. They spun and punched two more advancing guards. "Not the plan, but a good job." The guards went down.

Demeter raised her hand. She shouted, "It's time to get off this planet!"

"Now!" Circe hollered.

The prisoners shouted their approval. They moved around the bodies littering the Fight Zone. Guards, and some prisoners, sprawled across the burning sand. Those still capable groaned in pain.

Artemis fought with them. She started toward the Palamino but a giant arm grabbed her from behind. A hand covered her mouth. Demeter's back was to her. She was dragged away into the smoke.

The powerful hum of motors approached. Demeter watched two transport scramblers screech to a stop nearby.

"We need to hurry," she said.

More guards rushed from the scramblers. Half the prisoners ran to the outer perimeter of the Fight Zone where the Palamino sat. Sunlight reflected off its metal surface. The rest engaged in combat with the arriving guards.

The Pharon shrieked, fighting alongside the women. Her deadly tail whipped back and forth, lashing out and destroying the weaklings.

Leda used the hairbrush to smash another guard in the head. She called out, "Wait for me."

Beneath the sandy surface of Tartarus hid more than the tunnels and the giant vid-screen.

Thankfully, Enyo thought, the explosions had not damaged the access tunnel to the Star-Viper.

The Star-Viper was the warden's escape ship buried beneath the scorching sands. It held a crew of four, and only Enyo could activate the portal leading to the tunnel and the ship. The comm-tracker she wore linked directly to the security code, enabling her to instantly access the entrance portal.

Rex stood beside her, protecting her. She readied to descend the rungs when Cletus approached. He held Artemis around her waist. The girl tried to twist out of his hold.

"We're going too," Cletus said. His tone left no room for questions. He figured Enyo would make her escape once the guards fell. She was as cold-hearted as they came.

Without a word, Rex fired an enormous fist into the guard's jaw, knocking Cletus out cold. The guard fell back unconscious. The captain grabbed Artemis.

"What are you doing?" Enyo demanded.

"Securing some leverage." He pushed the girl toward the warden.

Enyo grabbed her with her cold, robotic hand and tightened until Artemis recoiled in pain. She smiled, watching the girl squirm in her bionic grip.

"Go. Now!" The warden pushed Artemis through the portal and followed. Rex gave the area a quick survey. Guards and prisoners battled everywhere. His men crumbled under the fury of the inmates. No one noticed them ducking into the tunnel. Except the Pharon. The beast shrieked.

Rex wasted no time stepping onto the descending rungs. He pulled the portal shut, securing the lock.

Cletus shook awake, rolled onto his side, and sat up. A crashing wave of dizziness broke over him. His jaw throbbed with a surge of raw pain. He shook his head to clear it.

What happened?

The Pharon's piercing shriek split the air.

Cletus looked up in time to see the giant feline-reptile's paw come slashing down at him. There was no time to scream.

The Pharon's claws sliced his body to ribbons. The ribbons fell atop the searing sands of Tartarus.

Chapter 28:
Feast of the Pharons

Rex clutched Artemis around the neck. He forced her down the tunnel after Enyo. The passage opened into a long cylindrical silo. The Star-Viper awaited.

Artemis resisted, but the big captain was too strong. The more she struggled, the tighter his grip became. She wondered if he could snap her neck with just the one giant hand.

Enyo halted. She turned to Artemis, grabbing the girl's right wrist with the robotic hand.

"Cuff her." Enyo sneered. "We don't need any trouble out of her."

Rex retrieved a zip cuff from his belt and secured the girl's wrists.

"Come on." Enyo turned back, punched a pass-number into the code pad. The Star-Viper's hatch swished open.

Near the edge of the Fight Zone perimeter, Demeter stopped. Although the blazing fires melted the last remnants of the force-shield projectors, she hesitated.

"You don't think they reactivated the force-shield, do you?"

"Are you kidding? Blew it up myself," Vesta said with a prideful grin.

"They didn't reactivate it." Circe joined them. She jumped past the perimeter line to prove her point.

"Come on."

Leda arrived with more prisoners. They bolted toward the Palamino. Circe opened the transport hatch.

Demeter watched the women gather and felt the chilly hand of dread squeeze her heart.

"Where's Artemis?"

"She was with us." Vesta scanned the area.

Artemis was gone.

Pharon shrieks pierced the heated air. The guards focused their efforts on fighting the creature. They blasted the beast's scaly hide. Blast after blast filled the atmosphere. The dust settled, and the smoke cleared. One beam blast was little more than an irritation, multiple beams sent waves of pain throughout the creature's body.

She lashed her tail and hissed. Her tail took out another guard, cutting him in half diagonally. The top half of his body slid off the bottom half. Lasers blasted the Pharon at full power. Her tail continued whipping about. The giant vid-screen exploded when the tail pierced the screen. Deadly shards of vid-screen rained down on the guards, but still they continued their onslaught.

"Hey!" Circe yelled, falling out of the way just in time to avoid being trampled by the Pharon's younglings. They bounded out of the Palamino's hull into the sand, playfully snapping at one another. They stopped when they heard the cry of their mother.

Bounding toward the melee, they quickly closed the distance. The younglings may have been clumsy and awkward, but they displayed surprising velocity and nimbleness. The guards never knew what hit them. They were mere playthings for the younglings. The younglings pranced about, playing with the guards.

Guards cried out in pain. The younglings batted them from one paw to the other, crushing their bodies, pouncing like giant kittens. One snatched up a guard in its mouth and shook the body playfully, tossing it aside where it landed in a bloody, lifeless heap.

Playtime continued until the remaining guards could play no

longer.

Mother Pharon shrieked triumphantly. Her younglings had done well, even if they did not realize what they had done.

"I didn't expect that," Vesta said, watching the Pharon younglings make short order of the guards.

"Get into the cockpit." Circe pushed her through the hatch.

"We need to find Artemis," Demeter said.

"We can't wait," Circe said. She helped the women into the transport ship.

"I came to get my sister," Demeter said. She surveyed the area. There was nothing more to see.

Artemis was nowhere in sight.

An explosion of fire burst from the sand near the center of the Fight Zone. The Star-Viper shot from the launch silo into the sky.

"What?" Demeter watched the small ship take flight. It was an escape ship, designed for stealth and speed.

"It's true," Circe said.

"What's true?"

"The Star-Viper. It's Enyo's escape ship buried under the Fight Zone." Circe heard the rumors about a ship beneath the surface. No one had ever seen it until now.

"Artemis!" Demeter exclaimed. Her little sister was nowhere to be found.

"Rex had a thing for her," Circe said.

"That creep." She hit the Palamino's side.

"Or she could be dead," Circe offered.

Demeter shot her a look. She did not appreciate her suggestion.

"Let's go," Vesta hollered back from the cockpit. "If we get in the air, I may get a track on her personal beacon."

Demeter glanced at the decimated Fight Zone. It was a smoldering ruin. The mother Pharon tended to her younglings, licking blood from their faces and bodies. The younglings purred, their tails whipping excitedly.

"If we don't find her, I'll never forgive myself," Demeter said. When the last prisoner was on the transport ship, she pulled the hatch shut and engaged the lock.

Chapter 29:
A New Regime Arises

It took only a moment for Vesta to assess the transport ship's control board. Demeter entered the cockpit. She wore shorts, polymer chaps and vest. Leda found a compartment full of uniforms and gear. The women stripped out of the flimsy gowns and dressed in the battle armor.

"You got it?" Demeter asked. She sat beside Vesta.

"It's not so different from the Wolfhound." The pilot kept her eyes on the vid-screen. She punched in the flight sequence code.

"Are you sure you can fly this thing?" Demeter fastened the metal latches crossing the vest.

"All these star crates look the same up front." Vesta concentrated on the controls. She smiled, pulling back on the navigational joystick.

After a bump, the boosters leveled. The Palamino left the ground. In the blink of an eye, they were airborne. A wave of turbulence rocked the transport ship. Demeter rode it out.

"But they don't all fly the same," Vesta said.

"Any luck locating my sister's beacon?"

Vesta scanned the readouts on the control console. She pressed a sequence of blinking buttons and viewed the vid-screen on the tracking dashboard.

"Not yet." Frustration colored Vesta's words.

Demeter watched the vid-screen. Circe entered the cockpit. She altered the gear by fashioning an armor vest into a bikini top and cutting a pair of tight-fitting pants high on her thighs. The tattoos stretching the length of her body weaved around her legs, disappearing into the black battle boots.

"We've got to get the gator meat to safety." Circe's concern was the protection of the other prisoners.

"We have to find Artemis." Demeter's eyes never left the vid-screen.

"I'm sorry, partner. If nothing shows soon, we may have to assume the worst." Vesta spared a glance at Demeter.

Demeter turned away from both women. She bit the inside of her cheek to suppress the anguish raging inside her.

A green blip appeared on the tracking vid-screen.

"We've got something," Vesta said.

"That means... she's alive!" Demeter dared speak the words aloud.

"And we have a way to track Enyo's ship," Circe said.

The blip blinked. Vesta pushed buttons, flipped a succession of toggles, and secured a lock on the Star-Viper.

"Let's go get her," Demeter said.

"Listen," Vesta said. "I'm an expert pilot, but this clunker is no match for the Star-Viper."

"Right. So, let's get somewhere safe," Circe said.

Demeter held back the urge to punch Circe in the mouth. The woman's insistence on leaving Artemis behind had grown tiresome.

"I'll send you somewhere safe," Demeter grumbled.

"What about all the other prisoners back at the prison?" Circe was weary of the bounty hunter's willingness to jeopardize all their lives for the life of one. It made no sense.

"I came here to find my sister, and that's it," Demeter said.

"Here's an idea. A compromise," Vesta said. Her eyes on the controls as she spoke.

She had their attention.

"The Wolfhound can run circles around the Star-Viper," she

said.

"So," Demeter said.

"So, let's go to the Barbera system, drop off the gator meat, pick up the Wolfhound and rescue Artemis."

"Agreed," the rivals said.

And that is how you devise a plan.

Vesta smiled.

From the watchtower, Eris watched the Star-Viper take flight. Soon after the Palamino followed. The Star-Viper moved fast. The Palamino changed its course once it was in flight.

No matter. With Enyo gone, Tartarus again belonged to Eris.

She no longer saw herself as a warden. Enyo stripped her of all the authority she once held. Too many years locked in the solitary block, hidden away and forgotten. It was enough time to reflect on her misspent life. At one time, she believed she was doing good only to realize she served the evil, wealthy scum ruling the galaxy. It was always about money.

It was time for a change. Time had come for a new regime to rise from the ruins.

She studied the vid-screens on the security console. It was over. The prisoners had overthrown the guards. The inmates successfully seized the asylum.

It was a time for change.

They were not prisoners. Not inmates.

They were soldiers.

They were soldiers in a new army. Eris would lead them.

Everything they needed to grow strong, the prison provided. It would not take long to raid the weapons depot and train the new soldiers in the art of combat.

She would recruit the Pharons, too. She knew they were not dumb beasts, but great, gentle, intelligent warriors in their own right. That was why she left them alone. It was only when Enyo and Rex started capturing and killing them that their fierceness revealed itself.

Her army would grow mightier than anyone could ever imagine.

When the time came, they would transport off Tartarus and start a new war against the oppressors of the galaxy.

Eris imagined herself in the head war ship, leading these galaxy warriors into battle wherever the oppressed cried out for help. Like the auburn-haired warrior and her pilot, the galaxy warriors across the universe would unite. No power would be great enough to stop them or dare stand in their way.

It will be a glorious day.

Together, all the women warriors would join forces and reach for the sky.

And if ever the opportunity arose, Eris would happily pluck Enyo's other eye from her skull.

Chapter 30: Score to Settle

The Star-Viper entered deep space.

Rex piloted the ship. Enyo hovered over him, watching his every move. She observed the coordinates he punched into the comp-control.

Artemis sat in the co-pilot seat; hands cuffed. She made no sound. The time for tears had passed. She felt only fury, but she had to bide her time. She knew Demeter was coming. The time for revenge would soon arrive.

"Where are they?" Enyo brought her robotic hand down on Rex's shoulder. The vid-screens revealed nothing.

"I don't know." Rex said. He felt the sting of sweat in his eyes.

"It's almost like they're ghosts." Enyo continued watching the vid-screens. She turned to Artemis.

"Tell me more about this sister of yours."

"You should know. You had her in your prison," Artemis said, her words bitter and defiant.

Enyo rewarded her with a quick slap across the face.

"Just answer the question," Rex advised her. This little chippy's attitude was tiresome. He would remedy that attitude when the opportunity arose.

Artemis heard the cyber-eye clicking, focusing on her.

"My sister is not a criminal. She's a bounty hunter. The best in the galaxy," she said.

"I doubt that, but that explains a lot," Enyo said. "And it gives me an idea."

Enyo activated the comm-screen. The picture focused through a haze of static. She punched in a code and Lawman Ena appeared. The woman asked Enyo about her emergency.

"This is Enyo, warden of the Prison Planet, Tartarus. I'm calling from my ship, the Star-Viper. We are tracking escaped prisoners and need help."

"We'll send a patrol ship right away," Lawman Ena said. "Shall we notify Her Eminence?"

"That won't be necessary." Enyo realized she answered too fast. She cleared her throat. "She is aware of our situation. I'm transmitting our coordinates. Enyo out."

Enyo gave Rex a shove. He fumbled to enter their coordinates into the comp-control. Lawman Ena confirmed receiving them, and the comm-screen went blank.

"Once we have reinforcements, we will make these ghosts bleed," Enyo muttered. A wicked smile touched her lips.

At the Ukan Landing Pad on Barbera, the prisoners filed out of the Palamino. Their faces flushed with excitement.

The Wolfhound sat nearby, docked where they had left it only days earlier.

Leda turned to Demeter when the last prisoner left the transport. "Thank you. I hope you find your sister. I really liked her. She said you would come."

"Where should we go now?" Elana asked.

"Avoid the marketplace," Demeter said. "Don't get yourself arrested again. Circe can…"

"Nope," Circe said. She shook her head.

Demeter stared at Circe.

"I'm seeing this through to the end. I'm coming with you."

Circe's tone said not to challenge her.

She pointed at Vesta and said, "I owe this one my life."

"She releases you from your debt," Demeter said. There was no time for this. They had to track Artemis and save her.

"Is that what you want?" Circe asked. She waited for the pilot's response.

Vesta looked at Demeter and said, "She's a good fighter."

Demeter shrugged and moved toward the Wolfhound.

"Let's get a move on," Demeter said over her shoulder.

"So, you're going with them?" Elana asked Circe.

"That's the way the meteor crumbles." She offered her ex-prison mates a small smile.

Aero stepped forward, Dhyana and Halla flanking her.

"You kept us safe. You kept us strong. You kept us alive. Thank you." The beautiful, dark-skinned woman nodded, as did the women on either side of her.

Circe was unprepared for the swell of emotion that overtook her. An uncharacteristic desire to hug each of these women overwhelmed her, but she resisted. She felt tears in the corners of her eyes.

Instead, she said, "Get out of here, gator meat. Be free."

One by one, the women gave Circe their silent thanks and then moved off. The women who became friends in prison paired up. Others joined small groups, and a handful ventured off by themselves. They dispersed into the world, blended, fell into the cracks. At that moment, each began searching for a new life.

Vesta touched Circe on the shoulder.

"Time to go."

"I wish Chrona was here to see this," Circe said.

"We'll be extra unruly in her honor," Vesta said.

Circe perked up and smiled. She swiped at her eyes and took a deep breath.

"Yeah, we will." She followed Vesta onto the Wolfhound.

Chapter 31:
Artemis in Peril

Lawman Dogen's black hair was parted in the middle. His eyes matched, and his jaw was chiseled from granite. Beside him, Lawman Graal wore her purple hair in a tight triple bun, one on either side of her head and one on top. Her features were no softer than Dogen's. They filled the comm-screen.

"What we're looking for is a prison transport vessel, Class B, the Palamino, commandeered by prisoners who escaped. Both prisoners are murderers." Enyo flipped a toggle and transmitted the information to the Space Security lawmen.

"Liar!" Artemis could not listen to these lies.

"Who is that?" Lawman Dogen peered toward the edge of the screen.

Enyo clamped her robotic hand over Artemis's mouth.

"It is a prisoner," Enyo said. "We captured her during the escape."

"She seems unruly," Lawman Graal said.

"You have no clue." Enyo tightened her grip when Artemis struggled to shake free.

Lawman Dogen looked at his tracking dashboard.

"Well, there's no sign of a Class B ship. There is a vessel in the area."

"Report." Enyo watched the lawmen track the unidentified vessel on their vid-screen.

"It's a solo ship, kind of beaten up, but really eating space," Lawman Graal said.

Artemis twisted free and said, "The Wolfhound!"

A shadow passed over Enyo's face. She pointed at the comm-screen. "Find me that ship."

"Orders?" Lawman Graal waited.

"We have reason to suspect the murderers are aboard the solo ship. Search and destroy. I repeat, search, and destroy. Use maximum force."

Lawman Graal confirmed their orders and the comm-screen fizzled to black.

"You can't," Artemis said.

The girl saw a wild glee in the warden's good eye. Even the cyber-eye seemed to whirl and spin in some kind of evil anticipation.

"I can and I will, and I will restore the rightful balance of power." She sat back in her seat. There was a burst of colored light. A million points of brilliant illumination lit the stars, growing in intensity. When at first there was nothing, there appeared an explosion of little pinpricks of light. The Wolfhound appeared from warp jump. It materialized dead center between the Star-Viper and the Space Security ship.

"Watch out!" Enyo cried out.

"Well, they know we're here," Vesta said. She was at home behind the Wolfhound's navigational console.

Vesta wore her own clothes, as did Demeter. The poly-armor clung to the warrior's body. Circe refused any of the garments they offered her. She preferred the makeshift battle garments she crafted from the uniforms on the Palamino.

"Let's blast them!" Circe said.

"That's a police craft," Demeter said. She acknowledged the Space Security ship on the vid-screen with a nod. "We don't want to kill the law. And my sister is aboard the Star-Viper."

"Then what do we do? Curtsy and invite them to dance?" Circe rolled her eyes.

"Great idea!" A grin blossomed across Vesta's face. She punched a blinking blue button on the console, then a green. The ship picked up speed.

Vesta steered the Wolfhound into a sharp curving sweep. She angled the navigational joystick from left to right. The Wolfhound corkscrewed downward. The Space Security ship tailed behind and opened fire.

Vesta dodged the blasts. Demeter strapped into her captain's chair. Secured, she engaged the drop-down gunner control panel.

The Wolfhound returned fire, but Demeter was precise to keep her line of fire off target. She just wanted the Space Security vessel to drop off. Even if it headed back for reinforcements, it would give them time to save Artemis and then warp jump somewhere safe.

"Can we open comms?"

"I'm kind of busy here," Vesta said. She guided the Wolfhound through another corkscrew maneuver. The craft swung up, leveled into an ascent, then veered around a fast-approaching meteor.

"Where did I put my bounty hunter badge?" Demeter patted her armor.

Circe saw the silver badge sliding from one end of the navigational console to the other and leaped to snatch it. She passed it back to Demeter.

Demeter pushed the gunner controls out of the way and released the safety harness. She rose and approached the console, then engaged the comm-screen. It blinked to life. Lawman Dogen and Lawman Graal filled the comm-screen. She was afraid the comm-system was going to go out at any moment.

"Hold your fire!"

"Surrender, prisoners." Lawman Dogen said.

Demeter flashed her bounty hunter badge. She held it long enough for them to run her badge number through their computer. They compared it to the information Enyo transmitted to them.

"This is Demeter, bounty hunter," she said. "I'm calling from my ship, the Wolfhound. You can verify my credentials with Lawman Jeb

Deering."

The lawmen scanned their readouts. Demeter heard a sequence of tapping buttons; a code sent. Instantaneously, a blinking green light reflected off the faces of the lawmen.

"Lawman Jeb Deering verifies you," Lawman Graal said.

"Good old, Jeb," Demeter said.

"You are looking for an unruly, on the Star-Viper?" Lawman Dogen said.

"Yes," Demeter said.

"Well, that ship belongs to the warden of Prison Planet. She has a prisoner on board."

Vesta glanced up at Demeter. She could see her partner tense.

"We know, and we are happy to escort the Star-Viper back to the planet. We can discuss the bounty there."

"Roger that," Lawman Graal said. "We've got another call, so we'll leave you to it."

The comm-screen went dark. On the vid-screen, they watched the Space Security ship disappear into deep space.

Enyo and Rex watched the Space Security cruiser curve left and blast off. The strobing blue lights were the last part of the ship seen before it was gone.

"That bastard is leaving!" Enyo said.

"Let me go. My sister will never give up." Artemis glared at the warden.

The cyber-eye assessed the prisoner with a clicking whirl. Enyo considered the prisoner. She freed her laser pistol and put it to the prisoner's temple.

"Then maybe I'll eliminate the problem."

"No!"

Rex rose from the controls. The big man paid little attention to the Star-Viper's navigational dashboard. He reached over, attempting to grab the weapon away from Enyo. She deflected him.

"What's your interest in this chippy?" Enyo roared. Furious with Rex's insubordination, she shook him off her.

"She's mine. My butterfly. You wouldn't understand." He

sounded like a little boy describing his favorite toy.

Artemis felt the icy prickle of fear run down her neck and spine. She watched. If Rex could overpower the warden, she may have a chance of getting free.

"I think I do," the warden said, her voice calmer. "She's special. You don't want me to shoot her."

She regarded the girl. Her head tilted to one side. She nodded.

"No, I do not," Rex said. For the first time, Rex sounded scared. "Fine."

Enyo raised her laser pistol and shot Rex in the head. The blast suspended him inches from the floor. His head melted away. Boiling flesh flowed off the skull like candle wax. The rest of his body followed. Bubbling flesh and liquefying muscles sluiced off the bones in a torrent. His charred skeleton fell to the cockpit floor. It sizzled, filling the cockpit with the most unhealthy stench.

Enyo took Rex's place in the pilot's seat. She glowered at Artemis. The girl was aghast.

"Rex messed up, and your sister will, too. I'm in the driver's seat now."

Chapter 32:
The Calm Before the Storm

"What now?" Vesta looked to Demeter for a plan of action.

"The odds are a little more even now with the law gone. Open comms to the Star-Viper." Demeter watched the screen.

Vesta entered the sequential series of buttons. The comm-screen blinked to life.

On the Star-Viper's comm-screen, Demeter's face appeared.

"Hello, warden. I would like to talk to my sister."

"You mean my prisoner? I don't think so." She studied Demeter. Her cyber-eye monitored the coordinates on the navigational dashboard.

"It would mean a lot to me. Maybe even enough not to tell what I know about Prison Planet."

There was a long pause before Enyo's response.

"Let me think about it," she said. The comm-screen went blank.

Vesta and Demeter shared a look.

"What do you think…" Before Circe completed her thought, the Star-Viper fired on the Wolfhound. Explosions jostled the ship.

Vesta regained control of the vessel.

"Well, that worked great," she said.

"We need to get Artemis off that ship." Demeter's mind raced for some viable plan to retrieve Artemis when the Star-Viper fired again.

Vesta responded. A quick spinning maneuver placed them behind the Star-Viper. Laser fire could not reach them for the moment.

"Just blast them! You've got that beacon to zero in on," Circe said.

"Yes, we do." A plan formed in Demeter's head. "And you're right. Let's use it."

"You want to return fire?"

"I want you to count me down." A wild glint touched Demeter's eyes.

Vesta understood what Demeter meant and grinned.

"What are you going to do?" Circe asked. The women communicated on a level that perplexed her.

"Five, four, three, two, one... now!"

A moment before Vesta depressed the blinking dematerialization button, a shock wave rocked the Wolfhound. The Star-Viper fired a homing missile, hitting the Wolfhound starboard.

The force jerked Vesta and Circe in their seats. Safety harnesses kept them from harm. Demeter stood next to Vesta, watching the comm-screen when the Star-Viper attacked. The jolt threw her off balance, flinging her backwards. She smashed her head against the side of the bridge wall. Her body dropped to the floor. The world was gone, and she felt herself falling deep into nothingness.

"Demeter! Demeter!" Vesta repeated in a near panic. She saw her partner collapse. She heard the sickening crack of bone against metal.

A flash of sparks exploded across the navigational console. A plume of gray smoke puffed from around the comm-screen.

"Circe!" Vesta tried regaining control of the Wolfhound, but nothing responded. Lights flickered and died. She pressed the green button repeatedly, but nothing happened.

Circe released the safety harness and crouched near Demeter. A trickle of blood ran down the side of her face from her hairline. She noticed the warrior's pupils rapidly darting back and forth beneath the closed eyelids.

"She's out cold, but I think she's dreaming."

"Must be nice," Vesta said. She jerked on the navigational joystick. Her effort resulted in a blast of sparks and smoke from the overhead control panel.

Totally focused on destroying the Wolfhound, Enyo did not notice Artemis slide from the co-pilot's chair. She crept over the remains of Rex when the cyber-eye detected movement.

Without looking away from the vid-screens, Enyo snatched Artemis with her robotic hand. She slung the prisoner back into the co-pilot's chair as if she weighed nothing.

"Watch as I destroy your sister, butterfly," Enyo said. Her words formed a snarl.

Pain flared through her back, and she let out a moan. Fear seized Artemis again. She was helpless to do anything against Enyo's attack on Demeter.

Chapter 33:
That Peaceful Place

Demeter found herself in that peaceful place on the cliff. An unnamed planet of beauty. The ocean crashed below. Waves pushed crystal blue water toward the rock facing. A gentle breeze caressed her skin.

The air was crisp and clean. She breathed the sweet air deep into her lungs. Nothing like breathing the stale, filtrated air when she traveled through space. She did not want to leave.

"There is still beauty in this universe."

The voice came from behind her, the old man. He did not startle her or put her on full alert. His voice was calming, and she fought the urge to turn around. Whatever this dream was, she did not want to awaken.

She dismissed the dream once before because she needed to stay focused. Now she focused on the dream and dismissed reality.

"I love it here." Demeter smiled. The breeze blew through her hair. The delicious fragrance of wild Lyssa flowers filled her senses. "If this is where the Great Reaper sends us, why is it feared?"

"You have to find your sister," the man said.

"I just want to stay here." Demeter rested her head. "I'm tired. I can't go back."

She inhaled the redolent aroma of the world again. It made her senses tingle.

"Rescue Artemis." It was the old woman. Her voice warmed Demeter's ears. Her tone was comforting, yet grave with urgency.

"I don't want to go back."

"You have great pain in your heart," the old man started. "I will forever regret planting the seed of that pain. It is not your time."

"We will be together in this place soon enough," the old woman said.

"All of us," the old man added.

"Are you…" Demeter could not find the proper words.

"We are who we are." The old man smiled.

"We are all energy, an eternal force in the universe." The old woman's voice was a whisper.

"No matter what barriers or dimensions separate us, we will always be one," the old man said.

Tears fell, and Demeter did not resist them. This place was so beautiful and peaceful, she could stay here forever. But she had to rescue Artemis. She had to go back.

Warmth and strength filled her heart and body when she felt their touch on her shoulders. It was like a blast of power, a battery recharge, an electric shock.

Demeter whipped around, but she was not quick enough. She saw the remnants of the couple fading away. The old man held the woman around her waist. The old woman's lips moved, but her voice tapered off, becoming more hushed as they disappeared.

"We will love you and Artemis forever…"

The beautiful world around her disappeared, and she thrust forward like entering a warp jump.

"I think she's coming to," Circe said.

Demeter groaned. Her eyes fluttered open. She touched her head where blood trickled from a gash.

"Help her up," Vesta said. Anxiety clutched her the moment Demeter fell unconscious.

The stench of smoke and burned electrical wiring filled her

nose. Demeter sat up and another explosion of sparks erupted from the navigational console.

Vesta was frantic, pushing buttons and flipping toggles, but the Wolfhound responded to nothing.

Demeter pushed herself up.

"Slow," Circe said. The bounty hunter paid her no heed.

Dizzy, Demeter made her way to the console beside Vesta. She wiped blood out of the corner of her eye.

The vid-screen blinked on and off. Vesta gave it a solid hit, and it stayed on. It showed the Star-Viper. The craft lined itself up for the kill shot.

Another burst of sparks propelled Demeter into action. She bolted to the ship's engine panel. Circe followed.

"What…" Circe watched Demeter twist the handle and remove the panel leading into the engine hatch. Smoke billowed from the opening.

"Give me a flash bar," Demeter said.

Circe grabbed a flash bar from the hanging rack, switched it on, and handed it to Demeter.

The light bars in the hatch strained to penetrate the black smoke. Illumination from the flash bar cut through the smoke.

"Hurry," Circe whispered. She watched Demeter disappear down the hatch.

"Prepare to bid your meddling sister farewell, butterfly," Enyo said. Her tone taunting and cruel.

Artemis struggled, but the cuffs held secure. Rex's smoking skeleton laid at her feet. Wisps of greasy black smoke danced atop the charred bones.

She could not bear to witness the destruction of the Wolfhound. Artemis spent her life defying her sister's wishes, doing the opposite of what Demeter always told her, and yet her big sister was always there for her.

This time, she had done nothing more than been in the wrong place at the wrong time. This time, Demeter would pay with her life trying to save her.

Artemis felt sick. Tears welled up in her eyes, but she did not allow them to fall. She refused to give Enyo the satisfaction of knowing she had broken her.

If miracles existed, she hoped for a miracle.

Oh, Mother of Many Moons, bestow unto us your cunning and courage.

The Star-Viper's combat tracker engaged. The weapon system locked on the Wolfhound.

Chapter 34:
Out of Hell, Into the Fire

The acrid stench of an electrical fire and smoke poured from the engine hatch. The flash bar shined through the heavy smoke.

Eyes burning, Demeter crawled to the source of the Wolfhound's distress. Her eyes watered the deeper she went.

"Hurry," Vesta called out. "Things are about to go ka-boom!"

Circe repeated Vesta's message.

"Roger," Demeter yelled back.

A burst of sparks exploded overhead and rained down upon her. She crawled faster through the narrow opening.

Almost there.

"It's a shame, butterfly. Your sister was one of the greatest warriors I ever witnessed in the Fight Zone. We could have made a lot of money if she just played along." Enyo glanced at Artemis. The cyber-eye spun and clicked.

"You would have had a good life."

"I can't wait to watch Demeter tie you into a knot," Artemis spat back. She was furious. She imagined breaking her cuffs and throttling the warden.

Enyo laughed.

"Your sister will not be tying too many more knots, butterfly." Her attention returned to the vid-screen.

The Wolfhound sat dead in space, helpless. It was a vulnerable target awaiting its inevitable fate.

Enyo entered a sequence of buttons on the dashboard.

A powerful hum rumbled through the ship. The energy for the Death-Blast began building power. Its intensity grew stronger. A digital readout showed power levels topping off.

A red button on the dashboard began blinking.

Armed to maximum power, The Star-Viper locked, ready to deliver complete annihilation.

"There you are." Demeter located the exact source of the damage.

An insignificant part crippled the entire ship, one tiny circuit board.

The last blast sent an electrical shock wave through the Wolfhound's mainframe and engine. It was more voltage than the samophlange processor could purge at one time, and it blew.

Demeter unscrewed the processor from its connectors. It was hot and burned her fingertips, but she ignored the pain. She dropped the smoking possessor and grabbed for the nearby box of replacements. Vesta bought these things by the gross.

She secured the new samophlange processor into its connectors. Full power returned to the Wolfhound.

"Go!" Demeter shouted.

"Go!" Circe repeated.

"Go!" Vesta responded.

Enyo fired when the Star-Viper was at maximum power. The surrounding darkness lit up. A brilliant beam of light burst from the cannon like a stream of liquid fire igniting the stars.

The Wolfhound disappeared before exploding into a billion grains of space debris. The fatal Death-Blast cut a line through dead space. It destroyed everything in its path. It missed the Wolfhound completely.

"What?" Enyo cried. The Wolfhound vanished! The bounty hunters and her former champion robbed her of her victory.

"Now!" Demeter cried from the opening of the engine hatch.

Vesta depressed the blinking green button on her console.

"You!" Enyo spun on Artemis. She could find no words. Fury raged throughout her body. She shook her robotic fist threateningly.

She stopped when brilliant luminosity engulfed the escape ship's interior.

Artemis fragmented into a million pinpoints of colorful light. The brightest light, the smile on her face.

"No!" Enyo screamed. She grabbed for Artemis, but her robotic hand merely swished through the dissipating image of her prisoner.

Artemis spent a good portion of her life traveling the universe. Everything she knew, she learned from those journeys. Like, for instance, it wasn't over until it was over, and that the force of good always triumphed over the force of evil.

The piece of knowledge she employed currently was an obscene figure gesture. It successfully communicated, galaxy wide, to friend or foe, that you just bested them. With both of her cuffed hands raised, she shared that gesture with Enyo.

"This isn't over," Enyo swore. Bright crimson rage colored her face.

Before disappearing in a last burst of sparkling light, Artemis blew the warden a kiss.

Chapter 35: Unruly Bitches!

"It worked." Vesta could not believe it. She double checked the coordinates.

"You got her?" Demeter was anxious.

"I did."

"Where is she?" Demeter tried reading the screens over the pilot's shoulder.

Vesta scanned the readout. "The brig."

Demeter made a face. "You didn't have to do it exactly the same as last time…"

Circe cut in. "Oh, please, will you shoot the Star-Viper already?"

The Wolfhound rocked from incoming fire, but the damage was superficial. The Star-Viper was at minimal power after the Death-Blast.

"My pleasure." Demeter took to her captain's chair. She engaged the drop-down gunner controls. Through the viewfinder, she locked in on her target.

Vesta maneuvered the Wolfhound into her trademark pretzel twist and circled around. Demeter fired a barrage of laser blasts.

In the Star-Viper's cockpit, Enyo cursed the attack.

"Unrulies!" Enyo tried returning fire, but the laser cannon was useless.

Her cursing continued. She tried engaging the warp jump. The vessel was unresponsive.

Enyo pounded the dashboard. The robotic hand caused more damage each time she smashed the console. Sparks flashed and smoke filled the cockpit.

The Wolfhound whooshed by, spun, dipped, and ascended. When Demeter locked on the Star-Viper, she let loose a Death-Blast ray of her own.

The comm-screen flickered to life. A static-filled transmission showed the warden in the opposing ship's cockpit. Her robotic hand raised and clenched in a fist. She screamed for the entire universe to hear her.

"Unruly bitches!"

She repeated the curse, screaming as loud as she could, until the screen went blank.

The Star-Viper's disintegration was beautiful. Blossoming like a flower, a great intensity of heat burst from its core. That intensity encompassed the entire ship, blowing it outward in every direction. Like the Lyssa flower blooming in the early morning, sunlight energizing its pedals to full blossom.

Fingers of fire stretched in every direction, the flames burning into nothingness. The fire sparked briefly and the Star-Viper exploded into trillions of minute particles.

Then, calm.

"Those are my kinds of fireworks," Circe said.

"Get Jeb on the comms," Demeter said. "We have to get ahead of this. We just obliterated a warden's ship."

Circe snorted and dismissed what Demeter considered a problem. Removing Enyo from the galaxy was hardly a crime, as far as she was concerned.

Artemis found her way to the bridge. She used snips to cut the zip cuffs and rubbed her upset stomach.

When she saw Demeter, she lit up and ran to her. They

embraced, all their conflicts vanishing. Reunited safely, nothing else existed at that moment.

"You found me, you saved me," Artemis said.

"Of course. You are family," Demeter said.

Artemis punched Demeter in the arm. It wasn't hard, but it was as hard as she had to give at the moment.

"Hey! What was that for?" Demeter rubbed her arm.

"Taking so long," Artemis said. "And everything else."

The sisters shared a look that said everything that needed saying for the moment. Demeter thought of the dreams she experienced, and the old people. She wasn't sure, but she knew what she suspected, and she wanted to share it with her sister.

"This is going to sound weird, but I think…"

The comm-screen interrupted her, sparking to life. Jeb's face showed on the screen.

"Demeter, I see you found your sister." A relieved smile fluttered on Jeb's face. Then he was all business again.

"I did."

"We've been hearing disturbing stories about Prison Planet Tartarus," he said.

"I can explain." Demeter glanced at Vesta and then Circe. They had her back. Circe placed a reassuring hand on her shoulder.

"It troubled Her Eminence when she heard about reports of using prisoners for some sort of kill games," Jeb continued.

"I see." Demeter felt muscles tighten in her back and arms.

Circe bit the inside of her mouth to keep quiet. She knew no one would believe her stories about Her Eminence.

"Yes, and about the apparent enslavement of the Indigenous species of the planet, the Pharons."

"They are a good species," Vesta said. "They deserve to be free."

"Her Eminence agrees. And she has issued a pardon for all the prisoners of Prison Planet. Those who remained as well as escaped."

Waves of relief and joy flowed through the women.

"All right," Circe said. "Good on us. Good on the gator meat."

Demeter said, "Jeb, that's great news, but we just blew up the warden's ship."

Jeb fell silent. He resembled a statue. Although he gave nothing away, Demeter knew his brain was working fast.

"Enyo was on it," she added, just so he had all the information he needed.

The silence that filled the Wolfhound's bridge made the air uneasy.

"This is serious, Demeter." Jeb picked his words with care and kept them succinct.

Artemis pushed Demeter aside so Jeb could see her.

"Demeter saved my life! Enyo had a laser pistol to my head. She shot her bodyguard Rex point-blank right in front of me."

"You will testify to that?" Jeb asked.

"To that and more," Artemis said.

"Let's keep it to this one felony," Jeb said. "Her Eminence would like to control the narrative about Prison Planet."

"Sweep the cosmic dust under the rug, you mean," Circe muttered in disgust to herself.

"So, we're free to go?" Demeter asked.

"Yes," Jeb said. "As long as Artemis agrees to testify."

"All right. Thank you, Jeb. This is Wolfhound signing off," Demeter said. She flicked a toggle, turned the comm-screen off.

Jeb's transmission faded. The comm-screen went black, and then bounced back on.

"Wait," he said, his image reappearing into focus in a burst of static.

"What is it?" Demeter asked.

"I have just received a comm-telex about an escaped prisoner." His eyes scanned the communique in front of him.

"A bounty." Vesta smiled. They were back in business.

"What does it pay?" Circe asked.

"I kind of don't want an escaped prisoner bounty," Demeter said. All she wanted was a couple of solid hours of rest in her own bunk.

"You'll want this one," Jeb assured.

He held up the communique. It filled the comm-screen. A familiar, ugly face stared at the women from the wanted poster.

"Kryll," Demeter said.

"That drug-pushing vermin," Vesta added.

"I want in," Circe said.

"Me too," Artemis said.

Demeter smiled. She looked at Vesta, and the partners shared a look. They agreed. It was time this operation expanded, anyway.

From one to the other, Demeter looked at her crew.

"We've got ourselves a bounty," she said.

The crew took their positions.

Chapter 36:
A Life in the Stars

The Wolfhound blasted through deep space. Kryll's craft was nowhere in sight. The tracker detected a ship, but the vid-screen revealed nothing. No Kryll. No ship.

"I don't see anything." Vesta studied her control monitors. There was only deep space.

"These are the coordinates." Demeter read them again. She clicked through the gunner's tracking field, each tick revealing the same void.

A missile hit the Wolfhound's starboard side.

"Where did that come from?" Cerci gripped the arms of her chair.

"Vesta?" Demeter's head throbbed from the fall earlier. The constant jostling made her woozy.

"We are seeing the same nothing out there." Vesta guided the navigational joystick slowly, keeping the Wolfhound moving.

Another blast shook the craft.

"Vesta, what's going on?" Demeter continued peering through the gunner's tracker.

"All right!" Vesta released the navigational joystick. Her other hand drawing away from the keyboard. She looked away from all the comm screens, eyes shut.

"What's she doing?" Cerci did not think this was the time to take a nap. "She's supposed to be flying the ship." She looked over at Vesta. "Hey, you're supposed to be flying the ship."

Artemis shushed her.

"Just watch."

Vesta's entire consciousness focused on the infinite space outside the ship. All other distractions disappeared around her. Gone was the clicking and beeping of her control console. The hum of the big thruster engine fell away. An engine rumble usually filling the empty passageways ceased. The other women's breathing on the bridge disappeared. None of it existed. She imagined she was outside the ship, floating in deep space, observing.

Something moved. It blazed toward the Wolfhound.

She directed the ship in a fluid movement, one with the controls. Vesta maneuvered the ship to the left, dodged the oncoming blast, turned and yelled, "Now!"

Demeter fired, blasting missiles into the vast emptiness.

The vid-screen revealed an impact on the surface of something. A ship hovered invisibly at their aft. Electrical bolts skittered along the craft's surface. They watched a ship appear in a shimmering array of crackling lightning bolts that revealed the entire vessel. It continued firing bursts of laser rays at the Wolfhound.

"Found him," Vesta said. "He was hiding."

"We know where he is now. Let's get him on the comms." Demeter watched Kryll's new ship through the viewfinder.

His grotesque, smug face materialized on the comm-screen.

Has he gotten uglier?

"Like my ship?" Kryll asked. He looked like a kid with a new toy. "It's new. Like my cloaking device? It's new too." He laughed.

"You know the drill," Demeter said. She peered into the comm-screen so the pusher could see her face. "We just want the bounty. Give it up, Kryll."

"Maybe you like my weapons better," he said, paying her no attention. "They're also new and powerful."

Kryll fired. Vesta maneuvered the Wolfhound out of the way

just in time.

Vesta switched the comm-screen off. She looked up at Demeter. They could still hear Kryll giggling and talking to himself.

"What do you think? Transport him back here?" Vesta asked.

"He won't fall for that again." Demeter's eyes never left the comm-screen. Kryll never stopped laughing.

"I have an idea," Circe said.

Kryll enjoyed his presumed victory over the bounty hunters. He continued giggling like a space academy boy as he fired repeatedly. When the comm-screen went dead, he knew he had them. He imagined the crew of the opposing ship crying out in pain and despair, begging for mercy. The image brought him so much joy he struggled to pay attention to the controls.

In a burst of magnificent light, Circe materialized in the co-pilot's seat beside him. He gasped. The warrior's body was a canvas for the most extravagant tattoos he had ever seen.

"Who are you?" Kryll could not keep his eyes off the woman's exposed flesh.

"Bounty hunter," Circe said.

Before Kryll responded, Circe sent a hard jab into his face. She felt his nose break.

Pain blasted through his head. He screamed out, dazed. The ship rocked when he released the controls to grab his face.

"Whoa, big boy," Circe said. She delivered another blow that knocked Kryll unconscious, then she took control of the ship.

On the Wolfhound, they heard Circe's victory cry.

"I guess she's one of us now," Vesta said to Demeter.

"And me," Artemis said. She appeared on the bridge wearing armor similar to her sister's.

"Are you sure you're okay with that, partner?" Demeter asked Vesta.

"A lot of scum in space. Somebody's got to catch them."

Demeter smiled. "Let's deliver our bounty and scoop up more space scum."

"Sounds wrong," Vesta said. She wrinkled her nose.

"Oh, yeah. But accurate."

An incoming comm-light blinked on the console. Vesta flipped a toggle. A good-looking man appeared. Firm jaw, crystal blue eyes, wavy blonde hair… Vesta recognized him.

She spoke to Dexter for a moment, catching him off guard by already knowing his name, then swung around in her pilot's chair.

"Incoming communication," Vesta said. "You're going to want to take this one." She winked.

"What's going on?" Circe looked confused on the comm-screen. Without hesitation Vesta patched her into the Wolfhound's comm-transmission.

When the image of Dexter blinked onto her comm-screen, Circe let out an appreciative whistle.

"Oh my. Now that is a man," Cerci said. "That is a man!"

"What is it?" Demeter asked. She was growing irritated. She wanted only to kick her boots off, take a hot laser shower and…

When she saw Dexter on the comm-screen, the irritation melted away. Her heart skipped a beat.

Oh, no! I'm a mess! He can't see me like this.

She ran her fingers through her hair, fluffed it out. She flattened the front of her armor, like it would help.

"Hi." He appeared as nervous as she was. "Is this an okay time to call?"

Hell no!

"Of course," Demeter said. She brushed a flap of hair out of her eyes, wiped her cheek and saw dark smoky residue on her fingertips. "No better time than right now."

"I sort of feel like it's not," Dexter said. There was an awkward silence. Demeter became lost in those blue eyes.

"Say something, D, or I will," Cerci's voice crackled from another comm-screen. Demeter slapped the comm button and killed the link to Kryll's ship. Cerci disappeared from the comm-screen in a flash of static.

"Come on," Vesta said to Artemis. She took the younger woman by the arm. "Let's get some tea."

"I don't like the looks of that guy," Artemis said. She was playing and would give Demeter the third degree later. For now, she was happy for her sister.

"So, any chance you'll be in the vicinity of the Astron Belt soon?" he asked. "I'd like to take you out for a drink."

"I think I can make that happen," Demeter said.

They talked for the better part of a quarter hour-cycle. Dexter asked what adventures she had been on since they last saw each other. She said it had been a slow couple of days.

He continued asking questions, and she deflected them with coy responses and a giggle until she had to let him go. There was a bounty to collect. Before she ended the comm-call, she promised to see him soon.

"You better, bounty hunter," he said, grinning. "Or I'll come looking for you."

Her heart fluttered. She wondered if she was blushing through the smoke smudges on her face.

I feel like a silly teenage girl... if this is how silly teenage girls felt.

Demeter was not sure. This was all new to her.

They made tentative plans to meet, then Demeter bid him farewell.

The Wolfhound veered to the starboard side. Kryll's craft sidled alongside it. Vesta re-established the comm-link with Circe. The pilot shared the coordinates for Sector Alpha 9. There they would drop off the prisoner and collect their reward. They would then file the paperwork to claim Kryll's ship as salvage.

They had a fleet to build.

Everyone strapped in for warp jump.

"Let's go!" Demeter exclaimed and the two ships blasted into deep space, becoming little dots of light in the eternal sea of darkness.

The ships disappeared in the blink of an eye.

The End... not even close!

A Note from the Writer

When I was seven, my life changed in the summer of 1977. It was June, and I knew all about **Star Wars**. Stories circulated about kids staying in theaters and watching it seventeen times in a single day! (Again, I was seven. I never stopped to do the math.)

I had to see this movie!

The day came and everyone in the neighborhood was going to see it. Everyone but me.

I had baseball practice. I made it to the All-Stars, and my season ran a couple more weeks. The kids smart enough to exhibit no talent for hitting, catching and throwing a ball had the rest of their summer free. They went to see **Star Wars**. Even my little brother went. Everybody who was anybody went to see **Star Wars** that day.

Except me.

I was crushed. I threw an epic come-apart. My mom was not having it. I cried, real tears, anything to get me out of baseball and to the movies with everyone else.

Nope. Didn't happen.

Mom promised to take me that weekend. Her promise was the only thing that kept me from running away from home that night.

For days I asked my little brother questions, but he didn't give much in the way of answers. He was five, but I expected more from him.

The weekend arrived and we were soon in the theater.

Everything changed after **Star Wars**. I abandoned my dream of either becoming a Harlem Globetrotter or playing football with my then hero Larry "Zonk" Csonka. I realized how reckless it was wanting to perform stunts with Evel and Robbie Knievel or hunting Bigfoot with The Six-Million Dollar Man and The Bionic Woman.

No, I wanted to be Luke Skywalker. I wanted adventure. I wanted to save a princess and be a hero. I wanted to go beyond everything I had experienced in my first seven years on Earth and blow up a Death Star. I wanted it all. **Star Wars** was my life for the next couple of years.

Back then, when movies were popular, they just stayed in theaters forever. When they did leave theaters, they were brought back for special engagement shows all the time, and I think I went with friends every time **Star Wars** returned to theaters.

Within a year there was a flood of sci-fi TV shows, movie rip-offs, comic books, and toys. It was fantastic! I was a nut for the Micronaut toys (which was also a comic book) and integrated them with my **Star Wars** and **Battlestar Galactica** action figures.

Then in 1980, **Star Wars Part 2** came out!

Ten was the perfect age for **The Empire Strikes Back**. Everything about it was bigger and better than **Star Wars**. For me, it is forever the perfect **Star Wars** movie.

By the time **Return of the Jedi** was released in 1983, I was thirteen and, honestly, I had been introduced to the forbidden fruits of HBO and Showtime. I loved slasher movies and action flicks, **The Jerk**, **Caddyshack** and **Porky's**. **Jedi** was a fine ending to the trilogy but was always my least favorite. (Once they made more **Star Wars** movies, it quickly jumped to my "third favorite.")

Three years is a long time to wait between movies. It didn't seem that long between **Star Wars** and **The Empire Strikes Back** because, well, **Star Wars** never really went away. It was everywhere. It was always back in theaters. It was a huge part of the late 70's pop culture.

Empire reached screens in the summer of 1980 and was a tremendous hit. It kept that **Star Wars** momentum going.

Twice, once between **Star Wars** and **Empire**, and then then again between **Empire** and **Jedi**, something wonderful happened.

Galaxy Warriors

Producers scrambled to find scripts to cash in on the **Star Wars** phenomenon.

This is where we started getting some outstanding low budget space flicks like **Starcrash** (1978) and **Battle Beyond the Stars** (1980). Since S**tar Wars** was a worldwide hit, these flicks came from everywhere.

Italian filmmaker Alfonso Brescia knocked out four **Star Wars** rip-offs in no time: **War of the Planets** (1977), **Battle of the Stars** (1978), **The War of the Robots** (1978) and **Star Odyssey** (1979).

George McCowan mixed H.G. Wells with George Lucas and delivered the Canadian made **The Shape of Things to Come** in 1979.

Although it was inspired more from **The Seven Samurai**, Japan's **Message from Space** with Vic Morrow and Sonny Chiba was marketed as a "Son of **Star Wars**" when it hit stateside theaters in 1978.

Disney released **The Black Hole** in 1979 and Aldo Lando achieved an authentic **Star Wars** feel with his 1979 **The Humanoid** by splicing in footage from **Star Wars**!

1980's **Flash Gordon** was as awe-inspiring to me as either of the first two **Star Wars** flicks.

Between **Empire** and **Jedi**, it was the same thing; one wacky **Star Wars** clone after another. The most notorious of the bunch was **The Man Who Saved the World** (1982), better known as **Turkish Star Wars**. (It "borrows" footage from **Star Wars** like **The Humanoid** did, but also copies every detail from the film.)

Ice Pirates (1983), **Krull** (1983), **Megaforce** (1982), **Metalstorm: The Destruction of Jared Syn** (1983), **Prisoners of the Lost Universe** (1983), **Spacehunter: Adventures in the Forbidden Zone** (1983), **Space Raiders** (1983), and **Yor: Hunter from the Future** (1983) all followed.

We're not talking about the artistic merits of these films. When you're a kid, quality is not really a criterion for your entertainment. Nope. It's all about keeping the party going from the film that started it all.

For me, by age thirteen, I was moving on to other genres. I still watched sci-fi flicks, but I leaned more toward the fun, cash-strapped **Star Wars** clones, or even better, the gorier **Alien** and the like.

Brett Kelly's **Galaxy Warriors** is a perfect tribute to all those incredible **Star Wars** copies that followed in the wake of Lucas's success. It didn't transport me back to the first time I saw **Star Wars** so much as it reminded me how awesome it was discovering the delights of **Starcrash** or **Star Odyssey** or **The Shape of Things to Come** on TV and video cassette. A lot of these films I enjoy more now than I did when I was a kid.

I fell so in love with Kelly's film I offered to write the novelization. He agreed. He sent me Janet Hetherington's script based on his story. From script to screen I saw how he achieved his retro tribute through practical effects, make-up, props, costuming, editing and design. My job was to do the same thing but with words. If you find some of my word or tech choices odd, I wrote it like it was 1979. Toggles were everywhere in '79. Blinking lights and buttons on spaceship control panels were the backbone of the genre. The idea of a "vid-screen cassette recorder" was really high-tech in '79.

I asked Kelly for permission to add little homages and in-jokes to those sci-fi movies I loved as a kid. He gave his blessing. Just about every weird name is from a movie. (It's up to you to now identify the movies these references are from.)

He allowed me the opportunity to take the story and make it bigger. He let me expand on the screen story to fill out this fantastic world.

I wrote the original novelization in 2022. It was to help Kelly promote the film at the different festivals it competed in and, subsequently, won awards in. I wrote it quickly. When the film was picked up for distribution in 2023 I suggested going back, polishing it up, adding some extras, and putting out a special edition novelization.

You now hold that book in your hands.

It was an amazing opportunity working on this project and having a very small part in participating in Kelly's fantastic film. The movie is a whole different experience than the novelization. **Galaxy Warriors** could have been made in 1979 and released in 1980, just before **Empire** came out. **Galaxy Warriors** celebrates all the movies, TV shows, comics and toys that came out after **Star Wars** changed the landscape of pop culture. For me, **Galaxy Warriors** is a very special movie.

In fact, I believe we "found" some vintage lobby cards from the film's original 1979/80 theatrical release, and proof it was released in Italy in 1981. Interesting....

I really hope Kelly revisits these characters and this universe again someday in the not-too-distant future.

Oh, and if you were wondering, I pretty much stopped playing sports after the summer of 1977. (I did a couple more half-hearted seasons, but it was obvious I no longer cared for the game. I had a new passion.)

Never again did I miss another movie because of sports or any other outside social commitment.

Robert Freese
July 22, 2023

Two copies of Lobby Card #1 were located from different sources.
The bottom Lobby Card shows considerable wear. (Canadian & U.S. Release.)

Lobby Cards #2 (Above) and #3 (Below)
(Canadian & U.S. Release)

Two copies of Lobby Card #4. Again, the bottom card shows significant wear. (Canadian & U.S. Release)

Lobby Cards #5 (Above) and #6 (Below)
(Canadian & U.S. Release)

Above: Lobby Card #8 (Canadian & U.S. Release)
Below: A rare Italian Photobusta from 1981.

About the Movie Marketing Archivist

Paul Mcvay is not only the curator of the *It Came From Hollywood* archives, but he maintains a vast movie marketing archive of materials that span the decades. His knowledge of esoteric movie marketing facts is second to none. He has contributed research to various projects, from books and magazine articles, to DVD and Blu-ray special features.

In 2022 he took ownership of Joe Kane's massive marketing archives.

He designed the **Galaxy Warrior** lobby cards based on 70s era lobby cards from independent distributors like American International Pictures and Crown International Pictures.

About the Writer

Robert Freese sold his first piece of short fiction to cult author and filmmaker John A. Russo. Since then, he has had three collections of short fiction published, *A Place of Dreams and Nightmares*, *13 Frights* and *Shivers*. He also contributed a story to Forrest J. Ackerman's final anthology project, *Forrest J. Ackerman's Anthology of the Living Dead*.

He wrote the splatter zombie novel *Bijou of the Dead* as well as the slasher novella, *The Drive-in that Dripped Blood*. In 2022, he wrote *The Brain That Wouldn't Die 60th Anniversary Novelization*. *Video Town*, a novella celebrating 80's Teen Comedies, about competing video stores during Halloween weekend 1987, will be out later this year. He is currently working on the novelization to **Splatter University**.

He lives in Alabama with his wife, Sherri, and their two deranged cats, Captain Howdy and Todd. He has a stepson, Jasper. He spends an obscene amount of time watching movies.

Milton Keynes UK
Ingram Content Group UK Ltd.
UKHW010714040923
428018UK00014B/789